Take Me Away

Everly Place Series - Book One

by Rachel Kirwin

www.rachelkirwin.com

Cover Design by Rebeca Covers
Book Design by Kelsey Clayton

ISBN: 9781070323619

Acknowledgement
For my husband, my number one supporter.
Thank you for believing in me on this journey.
I love you.

"Always remember that you are absolutely unique. Just like everyone else."

Margaret Mead

Chapter One

Do you ever feel like you don't belong? Not in school or in your family, but in the universe?

I've lived my life inside my books, inside my house, inside this small, pacific town and it's all I've ever known. It's not that I don't have dreams—I do. I have big dreams, but there is a difference between having a dream and a goal. I know that there is more to life, but I don't feel like life would welcome me anywhere else.

I graduate high school in one week, and while I can't wait to get out because I don't fit in, I can't help but wonder if I will always be stuck in this in-between.

Sitting on my bed, I look out my window and see the oak I planted when I was five years old that sets between my house and the farm. I remember watching it day after day and becoming so discouraged when it didn't grow. Eventually, I stopped paying attention to it, and it grew. Now it is this big beautiful tree with so many branches and leaves. I wonder if I stop thinking so much about growing up and my future if it will just happen. One day at a time, the way it's meant to be.

"Iris, your sisters will be arriving soon," I hear Dad yell from downstairs.

"Be down in a minute," I yell back.

My sisters are embracing this growing up thing better than I am. I'm so excited for Lily and Rose to come home for the summer; I can't wait to hear all about their last semester at college. I'm also looking forward to having more help around the house. Since Lily and Rose left, it's just been me and my dad. He works almost every day at the farm and I spend my days helping around the house and cooking.

Growing up in the small town of Leavenworth hasn't been extremely hard, but it also hasn't been easy. I can't complain too much because I grew up with parents who love me and two wonderful sisters. I have a couple "friends," if that's what you call them, but I have never really connected with anyone. Except Clay, but time changes people. I can only hope someday that time changes me.

"Iris!" Dad yells again. I throw down my pen on top of my notebook and jump off my twin-sized bed, giving myself a glance in the oval-shaped mirror overtop my vanity to make sure I look decent when my sisters arrive. I run my fingers through my hair, snagging them on a long blonde snarl and put on some lip balm before making my way downstairs.

"Dad, it smells great. I'm sorry, I lost track of time; I planned to make dinner." I walk over to the stove and lift the lid on a pan to see chicken and rice simmering. I inhale the delightful smell and put the lid back on.

"I thought you fell asleep." He kisses my forehead and the stubble on his chin prickles my skin.

"No, I was just reading," I lie, making my way to the refrigerator and pulling out the apple pie I baked this morning.

"And what book is it today?" he asks as he lifts the lid to stir our dinner.

"I'm actually reading *Little Women* again."

It's sad I connect to novel characters more than real human beings. My dad says I am a dreamer. I like to think I'm more of a realist.

"Have you been doing any writing lately?" he asks as he grabs a stack of plates from the cupboard. I help set the table with our old floral print china we've had since I was born.

"A little bit, here and there."

Books have always been my passion, but writing is what keeps me sane. There is something about the way you can escape into a novel and forget about the reality around you, but writing takes it to another level, because you can create the escape. You can go anywhere you want and be whatever you want to be without worrying about everyone else and what they may think.

"Iris, did you hear me?"

"I'm sorry, what did you say?" I lift my head to face him.

"I said the Kellers invited us over for dinner next Saturday. I ran into Mrs. Keller this morning at the bank. Clay and Luke came home from college yesterday; she thought it would be nice if we all got together."

"Daddy, please, no. You know that I can't stand those boys." The thought of them instantly makes my heart race.

"It's just dinner. Can you make an exception?"

I drop back down into the wooden chair with a sigh.

Growing up, the Kellers were our neighbors, and we spent our childhood fighting back and forth with those boys. They would always tease me and intentionally try to make me feel like I didn't belong. They picked at Lily and Rose, too, but not like they did me. Clay was my friend when he wanted to be and for that I was grateful, but as soon as his brother would notice us playing together, he would ditch me, no matter what we were doing.

I remember one particular Keller number with special distinction. I was eleven, we were all at the lake near our house, and—like a typical day—they were making fun of me for reading. Everyone was swimming and having fun, except me; my face was stuck in *To Kill a Mockingbird*. Clay, just a year older, came and sat beside me.

"I really like your dress. You look really pretty today."

My face felt warm and I knew I was blushing. "Thank you, my mom made it."

A boy had never given me a compliment before—except my dad, of course. It was in that moment my childhood crush on Clay took root. I looked at him in a different way. My stomach did flips, and I swear there were butterflies inside.

Just as I was about to close my book, I looked up at Clay and noticed his eyes were closed; his face was moving closer and closer to mine; my heart may have even stopped in this second. I shut my eyes, realizing that I was on the verge of my first kiss.

And that's when he stuck a toad on my head. Everyone started laughing, even my sisters.

"Knock it off, you guys, just leave her alone," Lily told them as she continued to swim, ignoring the tears in my eyes.

I ran as fast I could down the trail and back towards my house with my arms wrapped around my book—tears were falling, now, and next thing I knew, I was tripping over a big branch and hurling to the ground, scraping my knees pretty bad.

I looked up, and there was Clay with his hand extended. I placed my hand in his and he pulled me up and into him and he kissed me. Not just any kiss— the best kiss. I still remember the warmth of his lips and the way my stomach really did have butterflies in it.

Then he turned and walked away, and I was OK with that. I turned and headed home with the biggest smile on my face, completely oblivious to the blood running down my leg.

After that day, things were awkward with me and Clay. I felt like he was purposely trying to avoid me. I sort of missed having him as a part-time friend, and there were days I wished the kiss had never happened, and other days I wanted it to happen again.

Two weeks later, Mr. Keller was voted in as mayor of Leavenworth, and they moved to the other side of town. Even if it was only ten minutes away, it felt like more.

The day the trucks came and moved their stuff, I sat at my bedroom window and watched. Clay looked up and smiled and I felt that smile in my soul. It felt like a small part of my heart was going with them. I had never liked a boy before. I wasn't sure if it was the crush I had on Clay or the change taking place that hurt me the most.

The sound of a honking horn startles me, and I jump out of the chair.

"They're here!" I throw my hands up in the air and run out the door barefoot.

Lily and Rose just finished their second year at Bellevue. College has really been good for them. We all grew up pretty sheltered, myself more-so, and you could tell even by their appearances that my sisters had thrived while away. Lily and Rose are twins—you can't tell by looking at them, but you can tell by the way they act. They do everything together, so much so it is sometimes as if they are one person.

I run to the car and Lily opens the door and I jump into her arms. Rose joins us and we hug for what feels like minutes. Dad makes his way to the middle of the driveway where they parked their old white Honda Civic.

"My girls, all together again." He wraps his arms around all of us. *I missed this,* I think to myself.

After our reunion in the driveway, we carry in the twins' bags and throw them in a pile in the living room so we can go have dinner.

"There's a bonfire at the lake tonight," Lily says across the table, hunkered over our old family china, taking a bite of chicken and rice. "You should come?"

"Are you talking to me?" I ask, pointing at myself and then looking at Rose, hoping the statement was directed to her. But she was looking right at me.

"Yes, you. We haven't seen you since Easter. I'd like to spend some time with my little sister."

"I don't know, maybe." I shrug. The idea of a bonfire doesn't excite me at all, but I do want to spend time with my sisters, too. "Maybe I can go for an hour. I have to work after church tomorrow."

I've recently started waiting tables at the diner on Sunday afternoons. I'm trying to save enough money to buy my own car. Not that I have anywhere to go, but it would be nice to have something that is all mine.

"Clay and Luke will be there. We ran into Clay at the gas station before we got here. He asked about you."

"Me?" I point to myself again in confusion. "Why would Clay Keller ask about *me*?"

Clay hasn't even noticed my existence since the end of last summer. It was the day before he left for college at Washington State; I was walking to the lake to write a little, and he was texting while he walked in the opposite direction, and he walked right into me, dropping his phone. I leaned down and picked it up and read the words *I love you* across the screen. I assume it was to his girlfriend. He was dating Lexi that whole summer and I would often see them around, but we never talked. A smile here and there; that's about it. He didn't know, but I watched him from afar.

When I handed Clay back his phone, he made a little joke about my books and told me that I should really wear shoes when I walk on the trail because there was glass in spots from all the summer partying. And that was all. He was with his family at church over Christmas break, but he didn't see me. I saw him, though.

"He just asked how you were doing and said to tell you hi," Lily informs me casually, like it's no big deal.

It's not, really, to her. This is a small town, granted; everyone knows everyone. But why would Clay Keller bring up my name?

My stomach does a little flip, and those butterflies I felt six years ago return.

Chapter Two

After we finish eating dessert and hear all about the twins' last semester of college, we clean up the kitchen, and I go to my room to lie down for a while.

I can't shake the rush of Clay asking about me. I know I'm thinking too much into it, but it makes me happy to know he hasn't completely forgotten about me. Somehow, I push the thoughts to the back of my head and decide to get ready for the fire tonight.

Even though it's almost summer, the nights still get chilly in Leavenworth, so I grab a pair of jeans from my dresser and pull on the blue and gray Bellevue College hoodie Rose got me for Christmas last year. Sitting at my vanity, I throw my hair into a ponytail and call it good. Rose peeks around my door.

"Almost ready?" she checks, holding onto the threshold.

I take in a deep breath and my head is telling me no; my nerves are at an all-time high.

I say: *Yep.*

"Can I do your makeup?" This she asks with a smile on her face.

I shake my head. "No, no, absolutely not."

"Oh, come on," Rose begs. "You won't even notice it."

"Not happening."

Makeup is foreign to me. I haven't put anything except lotion on my face since I was a little girl and that was just playing around with Mom's makeup.

"Fine," I hear her yell as she exits my bedroom.

Downstairs, Dad gives me a lecture about making good choices and drinking. I don't know why he bothers; I don't even drink. (Last fall, after a football game, I went to a party with Amber and had my first drink of beer. It was disgusting. I spat it out and have no interest in trying it again.)

"You have nothing to worry about," I assure him, and sit on the couch to wait for Lily and Rose.

My dad and my sisters have always treated me like a little girl. After Mom passed away, Dad became more protective, and his rules became stricter. I didn't really do much, in the first place—but I did like to go for my walks down by the lake, sometimes not getting home until after dark. Even this worried Dad. He had just lost the love of his life, and didn't want anything to happen to his daughters.

I was thirteen when Mom got sick. That whole year is kind of a foggy distant memory that I try not to think about. She was the most beautiful woman I had ever known. Her heart was so full of love, and she had the voice of angel. When she wasn't taking care of us girls, she was volunteering at school or at church, where she sang in the choir. Everyone loved my mom.

When I was fourteen, the cancer progressed, and she passed away that spring. Even her funeral was beautiful; the whole town came. I stayed next to her casket during the entire viewing. I made a promise to Mom that we would take care of Dad. He told us a couple years later that he made a promise to her that he would take care of us, and he has. We all look out for each other.

"OK, let's rock and roll," says Rose when she and Lily finally come into the living room. I slip on my plain flip-flops and walk out the door.

Lily drives, which is probably best, because I imagine Rose will be drinking; she's always been the more carefree one of the bunch. Sitting in the back seat, I can't help but think about how different we all are. I'm the most reserved one—plain and blonde and, as you know, I don't like change at all. The twins are both brunettes, growing and maturing before my very eyes. Lily is very smart—she's more outgoing than I am, but not as much as Rose. Rose is drop-dead gorgeous and she knows it. Her confidence gives her a very *loud* personality, you could say. Our differences definitely show.

"Do you have any plans for the summer?" Rose asks me from the passenger seat.

"Just working at the diner. I think I may pick up a couple days after graduation. I want to save up for a car."

"And maybe a cell phone? So we can text you and keep updated on your life when we are gone." Lily looks at me in the rearview mirror. She's right; it probably is about time I get a cell phone, but I don't feel like I have much use for it.

"What life?" I chuckle at her.

"Oh, Iris, eventually you *will* come out of your shell and you will experience things you never thought possible. Just give it time," she swears with a smile.

Time is something I don't like to think about. It makes me think about the future, and it's something I avoid like the plague. With time comes change, and with change, you risk loss. Losing the people I love is a fear instilled deep in me. I still haven't even opened the letter from Washington State that is sitting on my dresser. Not that it matters—I'm not going to college this year, anyway. I need to be here for my dad. No one else is.

The two-track to the lake is bumpy and I'm flying all over the backseat. Lily and Rose are cracking up and I start to feel like Lily is doing it on purpose. My head bumps into the door window and she slows down a little.

"Gee, thanks for taking it easy." I scowl at her and rub my forehead.

"Sorry, Iris!"

I spot Clay's truck in the line of parked cars the instant we pull up, and I wonder if he brought Lexi. Even though I used to have a crush on Clay, he and Lexi really are perfect for each other. She was head cheerleader and he was quarterback of the football team and wouldn't you know, they were homecoming king and queen their senior year. It was only a matter of time before they ended up together.

Opening the door, I start to feel a little calm creep in. I'll stay for an hour and then walk home, I remind myself.

I recognize most of the people here from Cascade High School. Many are older than me, but there are few of my classmates about. With graduation just around the corner, I suppose there's no better time than the present to socialize. Most of the people here don't even know my name. They just know me as the quiet girl who never missed a day of school, except for the week that my mom passed away.

The fresh air feels nice and Blake Shelton is on a speaker in the back of someone's pick-up truck. Rose has already disappeared, so I follow Lily over to the fire.

"I'll be right back," she promises.

Great—now I'm standing here all alone right in front of the fire while everyone else is talking amongst themselves. I stuff my hands in the pocket of my hoodie and sit down on a stump.

"Long time, no see."

I turn around and see Clay standing there. His bright green eyes beam into mine.

"What happened to your head?" His thumb grazes my forehead.

"Is it red?" I ask. "Lily's crazy driving thrashed my head on the window." I run my fingers across my wound and return them to the pouch of my hoodie, wondering how bad it looks.

"Just a little bump. Nothing too noticeable." He takes a sip of his beer. "Are you ready for graduation?"

"For the most part. I still have to pick up my cap and gown and work on my speech a little bit more, but I'm ready." I notice Clay's gorgeous green eyes looking me up and down before meeting mine. I pull my eyes from his gaze and search around the party for my sisters. It's not that I don't like talking to Clay, but every time I make eye contact with him, I feel uneasy.

"I heard you were valedictorian. That's awesome," he says, and I nod, but honestly? I wish I weren't. I'm honored and all, but the idea of speaking in front of all of my classmates terrifies me, and the idea of my teachers pressuring me about going to college exhausts me.

Bryce walks up to give Clay a fake punch to the stomach before rubbing his fist on his dark, messy hair then loops an arm around his neck.

"Well, well, well... if it isn't Ms. Iris Everly. I've never seen you wear anything but those stupid cottage girl dresses," he laughs.

My face feels warm, and it isn't out of embarrassment but anger. Bryce Thomas has always been the class jerk. He seems to enjoy pointing out my clothing choices to the point of absurdity. (Winters are cold here, so obviously I wear more than dresses.) I was so glad when he graduated last year and I had hoped I would never have to see him again.

"Very funny." I roll my eyes and walk away. Why did I even come to this stupid party, anyway, and even if Clay is no longer my friend, why can't he ever stick up for me? I don't think Clay Keller has much of a backbone.

I spot Rose over by the music truck. She's dancing in front of a guy who's sitting on the tailgate, and I push through the crowd to make my way over.

"I'm leaving," I let her know.

"Don't go yet, Iris. The party is just getting started."

"That's exactly why I am leaving. Tell Lily for me." I give her a half smile and walk away.

It's dark on the trail toward home—about a fifteen-minute walk—but only a short while until the street lights come on, and I don't mind. I spend a lot of my time walking. Sometimes I just go out and walk without a destination in mind. There are days when I wish I could get lost with a book and a pencil and shut out the entire world around me.

Cars keep coming down the trail to go to the bonfire, so I stay to the side. I will never understand why people think this sort of thing is fun. It's loud, it's crowded, and everyone acts like immature idiots. I'm lost in my thoughts when I notice headlights behind me.

I turn around, but am blinded by the lights and can't make out the vehicle. Instead of passing me, it just keeps getting closer and then it stops. I hear a door shut but I still can't make out the person because the lights are so bright.

"Iris," someone calls. I shield my eyes with a hand and when he takes a step closer, I realize it's Clay.

"Clay? What are you doing?" He finally catches up to where I stand so I can stop staring toward the lights.

"You shouldn't be walking out here this late." He grabs a hold of my hand and leads me towards his truck. I shake my arm a little to try and pull away. Since when does Clay care that I walk at night, or alone?

"I always walk this late; I always have. What's the big deal?"

"I know but there are a lot of people drinking and driving and I don't think it's safe. Get in, I'll give you a ride." He opens the door and I climb in the passenger side.

"Including you," I inform him.

"Nah, I've only had half a beer. I'm fine."

I sit in silence in his truck and wonder why all of a sudden Clay Keller has taken any sort of interest in me. First, he talks to my sister about me, and then he approaches me at the party, and now he is driving me home.

Whatever the reason, it makes me smile.

"Here you are." We pull into my driveway and he looks over at me.

"Thanks for the ride." I smile back, and for a moment, I get lost in his eyes.

"I, um... I actually wanted to ask for your help with something," he says as he turns his head and runs fingers through his brown hair. Confusion sets in.

"What could you possibly want my help with?"

"I'm applying for an internship with the Department of Public Works and I have to write a letter of intent. I've rewritten it three times and the deadline is next week. What do you think? Can you help an old friend?" he hopes with a grin and tilt of his head.

"Yeah, sure." I nod and hope the hint of sadness I feel doesn't show. It all makes sense now. He just wants my help.

"Awesome, thank you. How about if I come by tomorrow afternoon?"

"I have work tomorrow, but I can meet you at the lake after dinner. Seven-ish?"

"Great, I'll see you then," he agrees, and I reach for the door. "Thank you, Iris."

Clay smiles.

I climb out of the truck and walk inside as his headlights slowly fade into the night. Dad is sleeping on the couch with a newspaper in his hand. I take the paper away, cover him with a throw blanket, and kiss his forehead.

I throw myself into my bed, where thoughts of the day keep repeating and I feel like a fool. Why would I ever think Clay had suddenly taken any sort of genuine personal interest in me? He just needs help with his paper. I should have known there was an ulterior motive behind him even talking to me.

I decide to quit feeling sorry for myself and get ready for bed. After putting on my pajamas and brushing my teeth, I grab my notebook, and write a little before drifting asleep with my pencil in my hand.

Chapter Three

A few hours later, the morning sun is beaming through my window, which is cracked open slightly, and I can hear birds chirping outside. I pull myself out bed and go downstairs to make breakfast before church.

Mom is heavy on my mind this morning. I'm not sure if it's because I graduate in five days or because she always made the best Sunday morning breakfast. Dad was usually hung-over from the night before, but today, it looks like Rose is the one hung-over.

"Good morning, Sunshine." I smile at her and flip a pancake.

"Ugh, my head." She puts big hands on the side of her face. "Why did you leave so early last night?

"I wasn't having very much fun."

Rose takes a seat at the table and I put a plate of pancakes in front of her before joining my sister to eat.

Dad and Lily finally meet us at the table, where we talk about the day and my upcoming graduation ceremony. He informs us that our aunt and cousin, Becca, will be coming into town Friday. I haven't seen Becca since last summer when she came to visit for a couple weeks. We're the same age, and she graduated last weekend. Unfortunately, we don't have many relatives nearby; it's a safe assumption they're the only family that will attend.

We all get ready for church—except for Rose, who stays put to recover. Once we arrive, I slide into the pew next to Amber and look back to see if the Kellers are here yet, but I don't see them.

After the service, I notice Clay and his family as we are walking out. Dad stops to talk to Mr. Keller and I stand there awkwardly.

"Nice sweater," Luke laughs. What is with everyone making fun of my clothes?

"Don't be a jerk; we're in a church." Lily steps in to roll her eyes at him. Luke has always been such a bully. Sometimes I wonder if he will ever grow up.

Dad finishes talking, finally, and I smile at Clay. "See you tonight."

He doesn't respond—just stands there, looking like he didn't hear me as he swirls his finger at his temple.

Not so different, I think, from his brother, after all.

I can hear Luke laughing as I walk away, asking him what that was all about, and Clay tells him to shut up but acts as if he doesn't know what I'm talking about. My heart sinks into my chest and I slump down into the backseat of Lily and Rose's car.

I replay the conversation I had with Clay last night to make sure I didn't take anything the wrong way—but he did, in fact, ask me for help with a paper tonight. *Why is he so cold to me in front of everyone? Am I really that embarrassing to me around?* My heart aches under the combination of anger and humiliation.

As soon as we get home from church, I grab a quick bite to eat and prepare for work, trying my waitressing apron on over my yellow floral dress. (*Sun dress*, not *cottage dress* like Bryce was saying. Asshole.)

"What was that all about at church? Why did you tell Clay you would see him tonight?" Lily asks, sitting on my bed while I brush my hair.

"It was nothing, just a misunderstanding."

"Those boys aren't being mean to you, are they?"

"No." I offer no further explanation. As we've gotten older, it hasn't been as bad. Luke was always the instigator of the group and Clay followed him like a lost puppy. Clay's teasing was pretty innocent by comparison, but it occasionally hurt my feelings or humiliated me, like today.

"Don't let them get to you, Iris. They are no better than we are." And she's right. They are not better than us. I'd never thought they might think they are, but now the possibility is worming through my head.

"Damnit, you're right! They are not better than us!" I vow this loudly with anger in my voice.

"Whoa, Iris... did you just say your first cuss word?"

We both start laughing.

"Can you drive me to work? I don't feel like walking," I plead, my hands steepled together like prayer.

"Sure. Let's go."

On the drive, I wonder if my sister and I have finally stumbled upon the secret reason why the Kellers have treated us so differently since they've moved. It feels seemingly obvious now. Clay seems to only be my "friend" when he wants something. Just like when we were kids, and his dad would drink too much and fight with his mom; he would throw sticks at my bedroom window to wake me up, and I would go outside and lie under the stars and listen to him vent. We were only seven, but even then, it was still my comfort he was seeking. And I always gave it to him. I gave all of myself to him whenever he needed anything and all I would ever get in return was someone who treated me like I was expendable.

As we near the diner, I ask Lily if she will take me to look for a cheap car sometime this week. With the cash Dad's promised me (since I'm not having a graduation party), I've finally saved up enough to buy. I hate accepting money from him, but I really want my own vehicle.

I decide to walk home after work. It's a nice night, and the sky looks beautiful over mountains heavy with rain clouds. I don't mind the rain; I actually welcome it. There is something about the sound of it falling to the ground and the smell of these wet dirt roads.

Feeling like a new person, and remembering what I told myself before work, I throw my arms out and quote Amy from

Little Women out loud: "I am not afraid of storms, for I am learning how to sail my ship."

A car flies by honking its horn. "Get out of the road," yells a girl.

I flip her off and run down the path to my house, laughing, wondering if I feel good or if I ought to take it down a notch.

Walking in my house, I'm still laughing at myself. Who have I become today? I don't know, but I like her. She (I) strut into the kitchen where Rose is cooking dinner. Dad must still be at the farm.

"Hello, my beautiful sister," I chirrup and give her a kiss on the cheek.

She, evidently not feeling quite as go-lucky as I am, wipes her hands on her apron. "What are you all giddy about?"

"I don't know. I just feel happy and freeeee," I croon as I spin around and twirl my dress, whatever kind it is.

I should feel like sulking after this morning's display of Clay's lack of brain cells, but instead I'm singing in the rain. He's shown me that I need to stop being a doormat to everyone.

Rose eyes me as I settle down to help her with the dishes. "Have you given any more thought to Washington State?"

"Nope. I'm not going to college—at least, not this fall. I don't even know if I was accepted."

She stops what she's doing and stares hard through her confusion. "What do you mean, you don't 'know' if you were accepted? I thought you got your letter months ago."

"I did, I just haven't opened it yet. There's no point. I'm not going to school."

"With your grades, there is no way you weren't accepted."

I shrug and try to change the subject to something about the rain we are supposed to get.

"Iris." She puts her hands on my shoulders and her face right in front of mine. "I know that you feel like you need to take care of him. I know you worry that he will be lonely. There is so much more out there and I know you have dreams that are bigger than Leavenworth. Dad wants you to live those dreams, and so would Mom." She hugs me tightly.

"Mom never left and look how happy she was." I put my head on her shoulder.

"You are not Mom, Iris. I know you want more than that." Rose stops hugging me and drops her hands back on my shoulders. "If you can look me in the eye and honestly tell me that you want to stay here and never have career or a life outside of this town, then I will let it go."

I look directly into my sister's eyes and I lie.

"I can fulfill my dreams here. I don't want to leave Leavenworth," I tell her.

We hug again, and I know she didn't buy it, but I need time to figure out what I want to do. Of course I want a career and I want to experience life outside of this town. I don't wholly know why I keep putting it off or why I am so undecided. But my dad really does need me—he doesn't have anyone else when the twins are gone. Until I know for certain that he'll be OK without me, I have to be here.

My future is a blank page right now; I just have to decide what to write in it.

After dinner, the rain sheets harder. My sisters and I clean up the mess, and we decide to watch a movie. I'm in the kitchen making popcorn when I hear a knock at the door.

"Iris, it's for you," Dad yells from the living room.

Who would be coming to see me at eight o'clock on a Sunday night, I wonder? I walk into the living room, and Clay is standing there with a hoodie over his head and blue jeans, soaked from head-to-toe.

"What are you doing here?" I demand, making my way over quickly to pull him out the door and onto the porch. The rain is really coming down now.

"You were supposed to meet me at seven o'clock at the lake. I waited for an hour but you never showed." He wipes his face with his sleeve. He sounds angry.

"Of course I didn't show," I hiss. "You made me look like a crazy person at church today. I would think that if you still wanted to meet, you would say something like, 'OK, Iris! I'll see you then!'" I shake my head and turn away so he can't see my face.

"I didn't hear you," he lies as his eyes wander without connecting with mine.

"How could you not hear me? I know you heard me. I was literally standing two feet away?"

"I didn't feel like hearing Luke ask a bunch of questions. He's been deep into my business lately and I'm sick of his shit."

"That makes two of us, but it doesn't excuse the fact that you basically mortified me in front of our families."

"I'm sorry, Iris. If you allow me, I'll make it up to you."

"What's done is done. I'll help you, but I'm onto you, Clay Keller, and next time, I'll call you out. I'm not the same little Iris that gets pushed around anymore." I try to sound serious, but deep down, I know I'm still weak. But I'm getting stronger.

"I believe you. Someday I will make it up to you, though, you'll see." He smiles.

A streak of lighting lights the sky, followed by a loud boom of thunder, and I jump. Clay places his hand on my arm and it directs some of that electricity through my body.

"Well, it's too late tonight. So, I'll see you tomorrow. Noon at the lake?" I ask.

"That sounds good," he tells me, and he starts down the steps towards his truck. "And Iris, I really am sorry about the misunderstanding."

I give him a nod and go back in the house. When I walk in, all eyes are upon me, and I don't really feel like explaining my late-night visitor, so I just put up and hand and say, "Don't ask."

Surprisingly, no one does, and we continue with our movie before going to bed under the last of the rain.

Chapter Four

I wake up early Monday morning and take the twins' car to pick up my cap and gown. Midway, I stop at a little coffee shop on the corner by school and get an iced coffee. I never used to care for coffee, but this past year, I have really taken a liking to it. While I'm there, I grab one for Dad along with a premise sandwich and make to drop it off at the farm for lunch.

When I reach the property, which is actually next-door our house, I find him standing there talking to the owner, Mr. Radley, and a couple of gentlemen that are dressed way too nicely for a farm. They must be making a business deal. I don't want to interrupt, so I just tap him on the shoulder and hand him his coffee and sandwich, and tell him I'll see him at home.

Walking back to the car, I stop and take a look around. At one time, this was our farm. I stop at the old oak tree I planted and run my fingers over the trunk, feeling connected to the changes that it has endured over the years. Where once was a fragile, tiny tree now stands a strong force of nature.

It seems like a distant memory—all the days and nights spent here doing chores and playing in the pasture. When Mom got sick, Dad didn't have the time or money to keep up with it, so he sold it to Mr. Radley. It couldn't have gone to a better man, though. Mr. Radley even allowed me to keep my sheep, Betty, there until she passed away two years ago. We used to visit all the time—at first—but after a while, we started going less and less until we never went at all, unless it was to see Dad. I was so grateful when Mr. Radley offered him a full-time job; if he hadn't, we probably would have lost the house, too.

If I push through the fog of distance, some memories are clear and sharp as yesterday. I can still hear Mom yelling from the gate to come home for dinner, and I can still smell her sweet banana bread infusing our home. Knowing I will never hear that voice again brings tears to my eyes.

I wipe them away and give myself a look in the rearview mirror to make sure my pain isn't noticeable. I don't like to show emotions. Maybe it's because—for my whole life—everyone I love has had to pick me up off the floor whenever I got teased or when I cried, and in some sense, I feel like I became their burden. Since we lost Mom, I've shut these feelings off from others, hidden my tears and bumps. I've needed to be strong for Dad, and my sensitivity isn't a weight he ought to bear.

The house is quiet, so I assume Lily and Rose are sleeping. I put the car keys on the kitchen counter and write a quick note to tell them I'll be back later. Then I grab my sitting blanket and I walk back out the door, toward the lake, coffee in hand.

The rain has stopped, but the roads are a muddy mess, so I stay to the shoulder since I'm only wearing flip-flops. I immediately spot Clay lakeside, sitting up against the big tree I sit by when I'm reading or writing. His legs are bent beneath his laptop.

"Oh, hey," he welcomes me, lifting his head from his computer.

I lay the blanket down next to him and take a cross-legged seat.

"Let me see what you have so far." He passes his computer into my reaching hands. I read his letter; there are a lot of grammatical errors, but the wording is decent. I can feel the burn of his eyes as he stares at me while I read. His hands are propped behind him and he looks more vulnerable without the laptop.

"It sounds good. I was expecting worse." I chuckle. "You may want to add something in there that explains you're pursuing a degree in Environmental Science."

We pore over his paper until we both agree it sounds good, and he shuts the laptop.

Clay makes a joke about going swimming as he looks over at the lake. I didn't bring a swimsuit—but even if I had, I wouldn't dare go swimming with Clay alone. It would be too awkward.

"How is Lexi?" I ask, curious if they are still together.

"I don't know; I haven't spoken to her in two months. Since she cheated on me," he adds, incidentally, pushing his hair back.

"Ahh. Sorry to hear that." (I'm not.)

We sit in silence until I finally break it. "Why did you really ignore me at church on Sunday?" I ask, picking at the grass to avoid eye contact.

He lies all the way back across the ground and runs his hands over his face. "I don't know. I just didn't feel like hearing Luke tease me." Those hands find their way under his head, pillowing it as he stares up into the boughs hanging over us.

"Why would he tease you about getting help with a letter for a job?" I wonder, now looking down at him. He is so close that I can feel his body against my legs.

"It's not the help he would tease about."

"What is it, then? Me?" I ask sternly, slapping my hands on my hips.

"Sort of. He's always giving me shit about you and I try to avoid it." He says this casually, like his words have no effect on me.

"So you try to avoid me because you don't want your brother to make fun you. Am I really that humiliating?"

"What? No!" Clay sits up quickly.

"Am I joke to you?" The anger prickles to wetness in my eyes, and I quail at the thought of Clay Keller seeing me cry. "Am I just that poor kid who lost the farm? The weird, stupid girl with the bad clothes and the dead mom?"

"You are..." A pause, as if he's run out of words to shrug me off. "Perfect," he blurts.

I turn to face him and realize, looking straight into his eyes, how close he really is. His face is only a couple inches from mine. I could bury myself in those eyes.

"*Perfect*? Are you trying to mock me?" I manage, still staring.

His eyes flick down to my lips and it sends a shiver through my spine. He brushes a strand of hair from my face and then turns away from me, gazing someplace far over the lake. "I don't know, Iris. I guess I just don't want you to think that me occasionally avoiding you has anything to do with you, personally."

I stand up.

"Occasionally?" I squawk and laugh at the same time. "You have ignored me ever since we were kids—unless there was something in it for you." My eyes lock pointedly on his computer. "Don't tell me I'm wrong. Or we wouldn't be here, in the first place."

Clay stands up, too, and grabs my arm to turn me towards him. "I'm sorry if I've made you feel... inadequate. That was never my intention," he assures me, but I'm not reassured. I'm confused with this whole conversation and by these subtle touches on my arm, my hair, my forehead. This is the most we've talked in the last two years.

Feeling a little brave, I pull away, and then I turn away. "Your words and your actions don't ring true. They never have."

I try to look down—to sink into the ground and cross my arms and anchor there, like a tree—but Clay puts his hand on my waist, and turns me back towards him. He rests his hand on my cheek and pulls my head to his and kisses me.

I've kissed Clay before, so I recognize the wave that engulfs my body, but that kiss was nothing like this kiss. It's hard and passionate. The sweet taste of mint on his mouth is inviting, I bring my hands up around his neck and tremble with delight. My heart begins to race and it lasts for what feels like forever. I want more, I need more— but I just stand there frozen in silence after he finally releases me.

Clay picks up my blanket and shakes it off before handing it to me and then grabs his laptop. "I'll see you Saturday?" he hopes.

"Umm… yeah," I stutter. "Saturday."

He walks to his truck and gets in.

I stand there, frozen, unable to speak or move as I try to comprehend what just happened and what this might mean.

Chapter Five

The rest of the week goes by slowly. I spend the majority of it working on my speech and preparing for graduation. As excited as I am for the ceremony, I think I'm more excited for Clay on Saturday. I can't help but wonder if there will be tension and awkwardness. Either way, I just want to see him and hear his voice. Our last moments together consumed me for days afterward until I felt like that love-struck child again, standing there in the woods with scraped knees and the ghost of a first kiss.

My family notices something's afoot. They ask me what's changed, who this new Iris is. I just keep telling them I am in love with life, which makes them question me more, until I feel like a character conjured straight from the pages of my books. I haven't read at all in three days. (I did, however, write a little bit on a story of my own.)

Lily and Rose are taking me to Wenatchee today to look for a car. Dad was a little skeptical—he thinks three young girls will get ripped off—but I know my sisters, and they have good bargaining tools.

The drive to the dealership goes quickly. I spend the majority of it writing and daydreaming. Adele's "Water under the Bridge" plays on the radio and, for once, the song makes me think not of novels but of my own life.

I can only hope that, if Clay doesn't have genuine feelings for me, he tells me honestly and lets me down gently. As much as I want him to want me, I would rather him be truthful before my heart gets too invested in the impossible.

We pull up to a used car lot, and a man with a big belly hanging out of his shirt and a beard approaches us.

"How can I help you lovely ladies?" He flicks his cigarette to the side.

I tell him I want to test the blue Chevy Malibu to the left, and he gets me the keys. Lily and Rose ride along. We agree; it's a good deal. The car has some rust and a lot of miles, but my price range is pretty low, so I can't be too picky.

After finalizing all the paperwork, I leave the lot in my "new to me" car, grinning ear-to-ear. Rose accompanies me because I am still a little nervous about the drive. I don't have much experience on highways; I usually stick to the back roads at home in Dad's truck.

The feeling of having my own car opens my mind to a whole world of possibilities. I am able to go anywhere I want, whenever I want. I crank up the radio and let out a shriek as I tap my fingers on the steering wheel.

"Let's go to the mall," I tell Rose, turning the volume on the radio back down.

"Ooh, yes. We can get new suits for the pool party Saturday." She claps her hands together before settling into her phone. "I'll text Lily."

Next on my list: a cell phone.

Rose informs me that Lily will meet us there. We stroll in and head straight to Dillard's so I can get a new dress to wear under my graduation. I settle for a white one with spaghetti straps and a floral imprint, paired with white sandals.

"What is this pool party you were talking about?" I ask Rose while we rummage through racks of one-piece swimsuits.

"The Kellers' pool party. After dinner Saturday?" She looks at me as if I should know what she's talking about.

"Well, I wasn't invited, so..." I walk away from the swimsuits.

Lily pulls me back to them.

"You. Are. Going."

I don't see why I would if I wasn't welcome, though. Clay would have mentioned it if he wanted me there.

"Iris, it's a small town. Everyone is invited. It's not like anyone hands out personal invitations," Rose snickers.

"Maybe you would know this if you got a Facebook account. The event has been posted for weeks." Lily holds up a neon pink bikini top and tilts her head.

I shake no. It's awful-looking. She puts it back and keeps pushing through hangers, yanking a light blue bikini, instead. I nod *yes*, and she hands it to me.

"For you." She smiles.

I laugh hysterically because I have never worn a bikini in my life. I am a one-piece wonder. But my sisters both insist that I *just try it on*, so I give them the satisfaction, and retreat to the dressing room.

The bikini's a little tight and not enough coverage for my taste, but I can't deny that I look pretty hot in it. I may not have much confidence in my appearance, but I do have a decent figure. I walk out into a chorus of the girls' shouts.

"*Yes*," they cry, "you are getting that!" Lily whistles, and I laugh. I humor them and buy the swimsuit, but it will take a lot of convincing before I'll actually wear this thing in public.

After we all check out, I am officially broke, and realize I need to pick up more hours at the diner.

When we get home, I am exhausted, and so spend the rest of my night lying in bed and mentally preparing myself for tomorrow.

A breath from midnight, I am drifting off to sleep when I hear a thud on my window. I ignore it and shut my eyes until it happens again. I climb out of bed, bedraggled from the long day, and walk over to my window.

Clay is standing outside with his hands in his jean pockets.

I pull the window open and lean forward. "What are you doing?" I whisper loudly.

"Can you come down and talk to me?" Clay stands still with both hands still firmly planted in his pockets.

I push the sill back down, throw on a sweatshirt, and leave out the side door.

The night air feels nice, with a slight chill and I rub my eyes so my sleepiness isn't too noticeable. Clay waits for me, and as I approach with my arms crossed over my chest, I tell right away he's been drinking.

"Hey there, old friend." He pats my back.

I smile awkwardly because I have no idea why he is here.

"I got the internship," he blurts the next instant, clearing my confusion, and throws his hands up so exuberantly it sends him staggering in an effort to keep balance.

"That's great. I'm proud of you," I shriek with excitement, and put my arm out to catch him before he almost falls.

The sky is clear tonight, and you can see the stars. The only light belongs to the street lamps down the road and a couple solar bulbs in the flowerbeds. I can smell burning and assume someone is having a campfire nearby.

"I couldn't have done it without you." Clay pulls me in for a hug.

I look around to make sure his truck isn't here. He most definitely should not be driving like this. "Did you walk here?"

"Yep, walked from right over there." He points to the left. "Or was it over there." He points to the right. "I don't know." He throws his arms up again.

"Come sit down." I tow him over to the gliding swing in the yard.

"I love you, Iris!" He says it jollily, jokingly. His hand slides around my shoulders. My goodness, this boy is drunk.

"What are you doing here, Clay?"

"You are the only person who never judges me. My mom, my dad, my brother... they all think I have to live my life the way they want me to. But not you." His pointing finger finally finds its way to me. "You've always been a good friend."

If only that were true. I've judged him many times in the privacy of my head, but he doesn't know it. I also don't think he realizes that he plays mind games with me that confuse me to the core. I'm not very good with words, so I don't know what to say, and to tell the truth, I don't feel much like keeping the conversation going with him in this state.

"Let's get you home." I pull him up and put my arm around him for balance as we walk to my car, then open the passenger door to help him in. "Stay here. I'll be right back," I explain, and shut the door so I can retrieve my car keys.

I should feel happy that Clay came here. He must have been thinking about me to go through all the trouble of walking over this late. Instead, I feel baffled. There are so many questions I wish I had the nerve to ask. Why did he kiss me only to call me a friend? Why is he going out of his way to see me at such odd hours? Does he need another favor?

Whatever the reason, I'm sure I'll find out eventually. I always do.

I go back to the car and get in the driver's side—and Clay is gone.

I search through the darkness outside the car and I don't see him. I get out and walk around the house, and he's not there, either. So, with nothing else to do, I decide to drive down the road. The thought of him being out there this drunk worries me a little bit. What if he falls and smacks his head or gets hit by a car?

About a quarter-mile down the road, I spot him, walking in the same direction I am driving. His black hood is pulled over his head and his hands are stuffed in his pocket. I pull up beside him and roll down the passenger window, but he keeps walking, so I drive slowly with him.

"Get in the car," I yell as he stalks on, kicking rocks along the road.

"I can't. You need to stay away from me, Iris." He's stammering and veering all over the road now. I pull over and get out, leaving my car running.

"Clay, stop!" I shout after him, hurrying to catch up. I imagine I look pretty ridiculous, chasing a drunk guy down the road in my fuzzy pink pajama pants. "Stop!" I say again, grabbing his arm by his sweatshirt.

He turns around to face me. It's so dark, but the headlights give us some light. He closes his eyes. "You're too good for me."

"What are you talking about? You're not making any sense." I'm still holding onto his sweatshirt.

"You," he sighs, as if by way of explanation, poking his finger into me.

And this is exactly why I've stayed away from alcohol. I can only imagine how crazy drunk-me would sound. The thought makes me laugh a little, despite everything.

"Just come with me. If you don't, I'll call your Dad." I pull him towards the car and—thankfully—he follows, but I don't let go because I'm afraid he'll try to make an escape. Not until I open the door and guide him in again.

His head lies against the window. He sounds faraway, as if murmuring across a lake. "Why do you even want to be my friend?"

Knowing that he won't remember any of this, I gather my courage, and ask him, "Why don't you want to be mine?"

"I do," he swears, lifting his head. "I always have." The weight of his hand on my leg is sudden and sad. I can't explain the feeling that takes over me. I try not to think too much, because I know he's intoxicated. I know I'll sound insane in the morning if I bring it up.

"What makes you think I don't want to be?" he asks as he traces his fingers on my thigh but I pick it up and drop it back in his lap.

"I don't know. Maybe because you don't say a word to me if you think someone might notice," I snap as I pull off to the side of his driveway. I dim my lights so I don't wake his parents.

Clay turns his whole body towards me. "I'm sorry." He strokes my cheek and his eyes are half-shut at this point. Drunk or not, the way he is making me feel is indescribable, and I fight it with every brick I've got in my wall. "I talked to you at the party."

"Yeah." I roll my eyes. "Because you wanted help with your paper."

"That's not the only reason. I like talking to you. You challenge me."

"I challenge you," I snort. Geez, he's really drunk.

"Yeah, you do. You call me out on my shit. People might think you are quiet and passive, but I know the real Iris." He smiles like it's some kind of honor for him.

"You don't even know me anymore, Clay." I look down at my hand as I twirl my hair around my finger. "I'm not the same girl I was seven years ago."

"I know you're not. The girl you were seven years ago did take my shit and she shouldn't have. The woman I'm looking at now is the one that I want to know more about."

He did get that right; I shouldn't have put up with any of it. I shouldn't now, but I am intrigued by this new man he's become I want to know more about him, too—when he is sober and makes more sense.

"OK. Let's get you in." I open my door.

"No, no. I got this." He opens his own door and stumbles out, bending down to say goodbye. "I'll see you tomorrow."

Tomorrow? *Graduation*. I really need to get home and go to sleep.

I don't bother trying to help him; I'm sure he has done this on more than one occasion. Instead, I put my head down on the steering wheel for a minute to collect my thoughts before driving home and going back to sleep.

Chapter Six

Morning comes too soon, and I struggle to open my eyes. The smell of bacon and eggs fills the air; I glance over at my clock. *10:06 a.m.*!

I jump out of bed. I never sleep this late. The late-night encounter with Clay kept me awake, and even on the clock, I take an extra-long shower to allow myself more time to process the last couple of days and to prepare for the next.

I'm so glad that my sisters are home to help with the cooking. It smells wonderful in the kitchen, and the sun is peeking through the clouds. Lily stands at the sink. She turns to face me with her hands perched behind on her on the counter and a big grin across her face.

"What?" I smile as I run a brush through my hair. My sister just stands there and continues to grin. "What?!" I shout, louder, with a chuckle.

"You know what." She points a spatula at me. "I saw you and Clay outside last night. Do you care to fill me in?"

"There is nothing to tell. He was drunk and needed a ride," I tell her casually as I turn around to avoid further interrogation. She lowers the spatula.

"Mm-hmm. Something is going on with you two. I just don't know what yet." Lily turns back to the sink.

"There is nothing going on," I scoff as I pull my hair into a ponytail.

There really isn't. Clay has been a little more conscious of me these last couple of days, but I suspect he is just feeling overwhelmed with school and this internship, so he needs someone to vent to. I don't mind being that person, as long as we have a mutual respect for each other. There is nothing wrong with a growing friendship. I convince myself this is our whole story—I'm no novel character—but the feeling of his fingers running over my leg floods my mind and I can't extinguish the glimmer of hope that this time, things are different.

My graduation ceremony is at four o'clock this evening, and I give in to Rose's pleas to curl my hair and put on some light makeup. I won't admit it, but I like the way the mascara widens my eyes.

Aunt Meg and Becca arrive about an hour before we have to leave, and I am ecstatic to see my cousin. Becca has always been like a third sister. Her parents divorced when she was young and she's an only child, so she spent many summers with us growing up. We reminisce and catch up, and I fill her in on everything that is Clay Keller. She is the only person I dare talk to about this because she has no affiliation with this town or his family.

Becca has changed a lot over the year: She sports purple highlights, a new nose ring, and a tattoo of a hummingbird on her wrist. My cousin has always been a bit of a wild card—you never really know which side of her you'll see. She is very smart, but also has a troubled side that stems from practically raising herself while her mom worked twelve-hour days. I'm not one to judge people on their past mistakes or their appearance, though; my opinion of people comes from the way they treat me.

"Any parties tonight?" Becca asks as she applies more eyeliner in front of my vanity mirror. She is a beautiful girl, and could easily go without all of the makeup on her face.

I question whether or not I should tell Becca about the big graduation party at Mark Sommerville's house tonight. I haven't decided if I even want to go. Mark always has raucous parties with kegs and a sea of people and it really isn't my scene. I know that Becca will thrive in that kind of environment while I'll be left twiddling my thumbs in a corner by myself. The only way I'll make an appearance is if Amber goes with us. Amber is a lot like me—a quiet introvert—but she has sharper socialization skills than I do.

"I'm... not really sure," I lie.

"There has to be a party somewhere. What else do you guys do in this boring town?" She rolls her eyes.

Becca is from Seattle, so she's experienced much more excitement than I have, and her life hasn't been all about family.

Aunt Meg is a wonderful mom when she's got the time to be one, but lately her career has become her priority, which often leaves Becca to fend for herself.

Defending our lifestyle and our small-town boredom, I tell Becca about the party, and she begs me to go. She's literally on her knees begging, and I give in before pulling her up through laughter. Now I can only pray that Amber comes, so I'm not a lonely loser tonight.

After reciting my speech for the tenth time, I put my cap and gown on over my new white dress, and meet Dad out front for pictures.

The gym is packed when I arrive. My body feels numb and tingly from the stampede of nerves. Our class is rather small—only sixty students at the most—but with so many families attending the ceremony, it's body-to-body in this small auditorium. The thought of speaking in front of the large crowd nauseates me.

But soon, Mr. Jones is introducing me as the valedictorian, and I'm making my way to the stage to give my speech.

"Good evening, fellow classmates. I am humbled to have the honor of speaking on behalf of the class of 2019. Today is a turning point in our lives. We have spent the last four years in the halls and classrooms of this school just to prepare us for this special day..."

I forge on. My speech is long but meaningful, and hope I have touched at least one person in attendance.

I close with a quote from Steve Jobs: "Don't let the noise of others' opinions drown out your own inner voice. And most important, have the courage to follow your heart and intuition. They somehow already know what you truly want to become. Everything else is secondary."

I choke on my words a little, but everyone claps, and I take my seat. I am still holding my speech in my hand and I re-read the quote to myself a couple of times. My heart and my intuition know what I want. But do I have the courage?

My name is called, and I walk across the stage to accept my diploma. That part was easy. I feel like I can finally sit down and breathe now that this is all behind me. Not just the speech and the ceremony—high school.

But the pressure of adulthood and the future replaces the anxiety of this day, and suddenly, it all feels so much heavier.

Chapter Seven

"I'll pick you up at eight," I promise Amber between a flurry of hugs and her parents' congratulations.

Over to my right, I see Clay standing with his family; his cousin graduated today, too. I catch him looking at me as they walk towards us.

"Congratulations, sweetie," his mom says with a hug. I thank her and stand silently with my hands clasped while my dad talks with them.

Clay is glaring at me with his hands in his pants pockets. He looks so handsome in a pair of black dress pants and a blue button-up.

"There you are," Lexi cries as she takes Clay's hand into hers.

I feel my body tense up and turn away as if it doesn't faze me. I thought they broke up. Clay didn't mention them getting back together last night. Did he see her after I dropped him off? I can't imagine he was able to hold a serious conversation at that point. I turn my head slightly just to see the expression on his face and while he looks annoyed with her, he doesn't let go of her hand; he looks into my eyes like he can feel the tension, and he must know I have questions screaming through my mind.

Becca joins us. She's glaring at me, too, but in confusion. I pull her towards the doors before she makes a scene.

Dad decides to take us to the diner to celebrate. My Aunt Meg tells a very long and boring story about her new promotion. Becca and I keep rolling our eyes back and forth, but Lily and Rose seem entertained.

"Hey, Iris." I hear a familiar voice. Eric.

"Oh. Hi," I echo as he stands over our table. Eric was in my graduating class. He must be having dinner with his family, too.

Eric's always had a little crush on me, but I've never seen him as more than a friend. We went to a dance together our junior year and he tried to kiss me; I turned away. He never held it against me, and was always very kind.

"Are you going to Mark's tonight?" he asks, pushing his glasses up his nose.

"Yeah, we plan on going for a little bit." I nod and look at Becca, who's giggling, and I know she's making fun of me.

Eric isn't an unattractive guy, but he is definitely not her type. He's tall and slender with black hair, brown eyes, and glasses. His khaki pants are too short for his long legs, and his light green shirt is missing a button in the middle. He doesn't always dress like this; I imagine these are special graduation clothes.

"Awesome. I'll see you there." He returns my nod and walks back to his table.

Becca starts laughing the moment he departs, and I shush her, glancing worriedly back to make sure Eric didn't hear. He is such a sweet guy, and I know all too well the feeling of being laughed at for my clothing choices and demeanor.

While we're at dinner, Aunt Meg gives me a graduation card with a check in it: two-hundred dollars. My jaw drops open. I know she makes decent money, but I can't believe she would give me this much. After trying not to accept it a couple times, I thank her with a hug, and tell her I'll use it to buy a cell phone. (Probably just a prepaid phone; I don't intend to use it often.)

We finish dinner and go home to get ready for the party. Becca opens her suitcase and digs for something to wear; she settles on a red and black plaid print skirt and a black tank top. I put on a blue sun dress, and she lets out a sigh.

"Iris, don't you want to try something else?"

I don't care what she thinks. I like and feel comfortable in my dresses.

"Try this on." Becca throws a pair of jean shorts and a white tank top at me. I hold them up and shake my head, but like my sisters and the unexpected two-piece, she convinces me to put it on. I'm starting to get annoyed with everyone trying to change my physical appearance, but I go with it, because part of me knows that it's time for a change and there is no harm in experiencing a new trend. I run a straightener through my hair and touch up the makeup Lily put on me earlier.

"Yes!" Becca endorses the look; she taps a finger on me and makes a sizzle sound.

Clay likely won't attend tonight—it's more for the 2019 class, after all—but knowing this bums me out a little. It's probably for the best if he and Lexi are back together, though. I don't care to see those two together right now.

I decide to drive and, as promised, we stop to pick up Amber on the way. Mark lives a couple blocks away from the Kellers in a big house on a lake. We all three walk up to the door, and I take in a deep breath before plunging in.

The music is loud, and bodies fill the living room and kitchen area. There is a couple making out on the couch and people are lined up around a keg in the middle of the kitchen.

"I'm getting a beer," Becca says, walking over to join them.

Amber and I continue into the living room where there is dancing and a crowd around the dining room table, playing drinking games.

"Hello again." Eric hands me a red cup.

"What's this?" I bring it to my nose to smell it. Beer. I hand it back. "No, thank you. I drove, so I'm not drinking."

"Oh, come on. You have to celebrate. You just finished high school." He throws his hands up, splashing the contents of his cup, and lets out a shouted *woo-hoo*! I've never imagined Eric as a drinker, but it looks like it's helping him to loosen up. He takes the beer back when I offer it again.

I look over and see Clay, Bryce, his girlfriend, and Lexi walk through the door. I should have guessed they'd show up.

I grab the drink back from Eric and chug it, gagging a little, but not letting it stop me. While I drink, I make eye contact with Clay. He stands there in amazement at the sight of quiet little Iris slamming a beer and wearing booty shorts with makeup on and my hair down—it's something I can't quite believe, myself.

"You're driving." I point to Amber and laugh. She doesn't drink, anyways—but then again, neither do I.

Lexi is trying to pull Clay into the kitchen, but he frees his arm and she goes without him. He's coming this way. *He's coming this way*. I choke down the malty bitterness while trying to hold my composure. I need another beer. My heart is racing and I'm getting nervous.

"Eric, can you get me another?" I hand him my cup.

He grabs it from me. "Hell, yes!"

I turn to make conversation with Amber so I'm not just standing here like I'm waiting for him to approach me. And... he doesn't. He walks right past me, brushing his side against mine with a half-smile and a nod, and he heads to the table where there is a serious game of tippy cup underway.

A nod. After these last couple days, all I get is a nod?

Eric reemerges from the crowd with my drink and I thank him for it. Becca is still in the kitchen flirting with a couple of guys from the baseball team. I look back over to Clay as Lexi walks up beside to kiss him on the cheek. He doesn't seem to acknowledge her existence, which surprises me. At least it's not just me that he ignores. If this is the way he treats the women he claims to care about, I want no part of it. It still stings a little, but I slam my second beer and the pain begins to subside.

"Whoa. Killer." Eric takes my beer from me.

"Hey," I stammer, "I was drinking that."

"You need to pace yourself. I said we needed to *celebrate,* not annihilate," he laughs, handing my drink back.

I take a sip in agreement and my eyes wander back to the table. Clay is partaking in the game now, trying to flip a cup upside-down while Lexi cheers him on. He finally gets it, and high on victory, he grabs her face and pulls it to his. He kisses her. I shake my cup and realize my beer is gone.

"Refill." I mean to hand it to Eric, but Amber swoops in and says she'll get it for me.

I sit down on the couch and begin to feel the burn in my chest from the beer, which is allowing me to loosen up a bit more. Eric takes a seat beside me, and I give Clay and Lexi one more vile look before thinking *two can play this game.*

I'm not even sure if there is a game, but my head tells me there is, so I scoot over and sit across Eric's lap. His face is inches from mine, and I hope that he doesn't get the wrong idea and try to kiss me again. I can smell the alcohol on his breath; he has a small bottle of liquor in hand he keeps sipping on.

Becca and Amber come over to us, and Becca looks confused. She is gesturing her hands back and forth from me to Clay and I just shake my head. Then Amber hands me my drink, and Becca gets even more confused.

"What has gotten into you, Iris? I like it." She gives a smile and an evil laugh.

Feeling pretty good now and knowing I don't want this confidence to fade just yet, I grab the bottle from Eric and take a sip only to spit it out.

"It's an acquired taste," he fobs, taking another swig.

I'm not sure if it's my loud laughter or Becca's dancing that catches Clay's attention, but he walks over to us. I ignore him just to give him a taste of his own medicine.

"Iris, can I talk to you?" he asks, but I continue to ignore him.

I'm still sitting on Eric's lap, but Clay walks over to me and kneels down so his face is level with mine. "Iris, I said *can I talk to you*." His eyes are still gorgeous. But today, I won't go swimming in them—today, I'm pretty upset.

"Oh, I'm sorry, the music is loud and I didn't know you would actually want to talk to me in *public*." I glance around flippantly, and then bring my eyes back to his with a serious look on my face.

"Are you drunk?" He should know that I am. And he was right, that night in my new car, drunk out of his mind—this is not the Iris he grew up knowing, but I kind of like this side of me. She's happy and doesn't care what anyone else thinks.

"Maybe a little." I pinch my fingers a quarter-inch part and squint my eyes through them.

"Come on." Becca pushes her way between me and Clay, almost knocking him over. "We are going down to the lake to go swimming."

"I don't want to go. I want more of this." I swish my cup up as I'm pulled to my feet.

"They have some." She points to the boys she was talking to in the kitchen.

I shrug *OK*.

"Didn't you drive?" Clay asks while he helps me balance. I can't understand why he is acting so concerned. "I saw your car out front."

"I did, but we are just walking down to the lake. Besides, my best friend is driving later." I put my arm around Amber's shoulder and we turn away from him. I notice Lexi walking back and forth from the kitchen to the living room and point. "Your girlfriend's looking for you."

“Come on, Eric; you can walk down with us," I call out with my arm still hanging around Amber's neck. He jumps off the couch and hurries over to us like he was waiting for an invitation.

We all gather outside to walk down to Mark's lakefront property, including a few guys I don't know. (Becca sure knows how to reel them in.) I'm a little sad we're leaving the party, but I feel thrilled I was able to catch Clay's attention, and in front of a crowd.

Sam's already there, passing beer on the grass.

Now what? I wonder. What do kids my age do at the lake at night without a book or writing pad?

A guy I don't recognize is working on starting a fire, I think I hear someone call him Kyle. Meanwhile, a few more stragglers wander down, including two girls from my class and another stranger.

I keep sipping, and it takes me a good hour to finish this beer. I am enjoying sitting by the fire and being social. This is all new to me, and even though it's not something I want to do often, I can see why people find this entertaining. I may feel differently tomorrow when I wake up, of course, but right now I am finding comfort and courage in this beverage and the calm of the fire.

I talk with Amber around the fire as the group holds their cups high and sings-along with Garth Brooks, worrying that she feels left out. And then Becca reiterates her stupid idea that we all go swimming. Fearless, now, I oblige.

We run down to the lake, laughing and stumbling all over. Becca bares all and before jumping in. It's dark enough that you can't see much, but she still has more guts than I do. A couple guys jump in with their boxers on and I decide to venture out with just my shorts and bra; the alcohol has removed any trace of shame I might otherwise feel over my body. Amber sits on a stump, looking very unamused.

Eric yells to me from the water. "Come on, Iris, jump in!"

I'm ready to go, too, when I feel a hand grab ahold of my arm.

"What the hell are you doing? What's gotten into you?" I recognize that voice.

I turn around to face Clay.

"I don't think that's any of your business." I yank my arm away from him and fall backwards.

"Damnit, Iris, you're wasted." He helps me back to my feet. Somewhere under the miasma of cheap beer, I am distantly aware that I'm barely dressed. Eric yells again, but I ignore him.

"Who is that?" Clay asks.

I'm eighteen years old; I can do whatever I want. Who does this guy think he is? All of a sudden, he pops back into my life and acts like I owe him an explanation for my actions.

"That's Eric, and I'm going swimming with him." I smile.

"Let me take you home." Clay places his hand on my arm again. His touch ripples through my body and I want more than anything to kiss those lips again.

"Where is Lexi?" I dare as I cross my arms and try to hide my cleavage. I suddenly feel very exposed.

"I don't know; probably in Mark's house still." He settles his hand behind my back and pulls me closer to him to brace me while I stumble around.

"Why would you leave your girlfriend to come here and harass me?" I look at the water. Everyone is getting out now, so I pull away from Clay and put my shirt back on. I'm certainly not swimming by myself.

"Girlfriend? I thought I told you..."

"Everything OK?" Eric interrupts, walking over to us and pulling his shirt over his head.

"Yes," I tell him, and grab Eric's arm to lead him back to the fire. "Clay was just leaving."

But Clay doesn't leave; he follows us. Eric grabs a beer from the case and hands me one. I open the bottle and take a drink, and Clay snatches it out of my hand.

"What the hell?" I demand before laughing at myself. "I just said *hell*."

Still laughing. Did I say that out loud? I can't remember. I wrench my bottle back from Clay and Eric steps in.

"Just let the girl drink and have a little fun." He gives him a little shove. I'm pretty impressed with Eric right now; he's usually very calm and collected, but then again, so am I.

"With you? Not a chance." Clay shoves him back, knocking him to the ground.

This is new: two guys fighting over my attention. I'm not sure what they are really fighting about, but to put an early end to it, I agree to leave with Clay. I want to talk to him, anyways, since I probably won't remember tomorrow and I'm still feeling pretty bold.

I don't feel comfortable leaving Becca here on her own, so I tempt my cousin with the promise of drinking a beer together in the pole-barn, and meanwhile convince her to ride home with Amber in my car. Lastly, I sneak a couple of beers from the case and hurry to Clay's truck.

I like the feeling of being sneaky a little too much, I discover. Usually my adrenaline rushes are from reading about something exciting and adventurous; now I am experiencing it.

"I needed this," I confess to Clay as we pull away from the lake and I hug the two beers in my lap.

"I'm glad you had fun." He glances over at me with a smile. I wonder how much he has had to drink. I didn't even think about it before getting in the car with him, but he doesn't seem drunk at all. How the tables have turned.

"Why are you so angry with me?" I ask.

"I'm not angry; I'm just worried." He has one hand on the steering wheel and the other is brushing his fingers through his hair.

I give him a confused look.

"You never drink and you have drunk quite a bit tonight. I don't want you to do anything you regret." I roll my eyes.

I have him pull over a few yards before my house so that we can walk up without Dad and Aunt Meg knowing about it. The clock on Clay's truck says 1:10 a.m. We're home before my two o'clock curfew, and so are Becca and Amber; I spot them on the porch swing.

"So, all you wanted to do was pull me away from having fun, and you drop me off at home so I can be a good little girl?" I ask him, still wondering what his motive here is.

"I wanted to make sure you got home safe. You aren't used to drinking like that and I don't trust those guys—especially that Eric kid."

I burst out laughing. "*Eric*? You seriously think Eric is a threat to me?"

"Hey, now, it's the quiet ones you have to watch out for." He gives me a wink. I don't know how to take that statement, so for lack of anything smarter to say, I put my head down on the dash, trying not to make eye contact.

"What's going on with you and Lexi?"

"Nothing. I told you we broke up."

"It didn't look that way to me."

"She doesn't seem to get it. I keep telling her we can't fix it but she keeps trying." He lays his own head back on the rest.

"Probably because you give her mixed signals. If I broke up with someone, I certainly wouldn't be kissing them at a party." I shake my head in disbelief at his antics with women.

"It was a reaction." He brushes it off. I wonder if he plays games with her the way that he does with me. Either way, I still want to find out what grown-up Clay is all about; maybe when I do, this will all make more sense.

"Come with us," I tell him with a smile.

He smiles back. "All right. I can hang out for a few minutes."

Becca and Amber must have grown tired of waiting, because they're no longer outside and I see the light in my bedroom on. I'm glad Clay is here, though. It's nice being able to interact with him and not feel like his brother is going to come drag him away and make fun of me.

Minutes turn into hours of talking and laughing on the porch swing, and I've fairly sobered up at this point. Even though I'm no longer drunk, I'm surprised to find myself feeling more comfortable with Clay than I have for years. We talk about his new internship and he tells me about how college isn't at all what he expected and how he really messed up his first year. I tell him I'm considering putting off college for a while and staying home to help my dad.

"I thought you planned on going to State?" He looks surprised.

I really don't feel like explaining myself to him, so I just go with it.

"I am. I've just been contemplating whether or not I should wait until second semester." The truth is, I have no intentions of going to State. Even if I did go to school, I would prefer community college versus a university. I know I have the brains for a bigger and better school, but I don't have the socialization, a degree is a degree, and the introvert in me says *smaller is better*.

"I personally wouldn't put it off. You'll feel more comfortable starting with all the freshmen at the same time rather than coming in late."

"I just need to make sure my dad is OK before I make any decisions."

This conversation makes me uneasy. I've had it so many times with Dad, my sister, my teachers. I wish everyone would just leave it alone.

"You can't put your dreams on hold just because you're scared to leave this town. If you let life pass you by, you are going to resent the people you feel are holding you back."

"I'm not scared to leave. Well, maybe a little. This town is all I know and the world is big and cruel. But my main concern is my dad and his well-being. We girls are all he has." I shrug.

When did Clay Keller become so deep? I understand what he says, but he doesn't understand the way I feel. No one does. I don't like where this is going; I need to change the subject before I start getting emotional.

"What time is it?" I stand up, suddenly realizing it's almost morning.

Clay reaches his hand in his pocket and pulls out his phone. "4:30." His eyes widen. "Let's watch the sunrise."

I wasn't expecting that. As much as I would love for this night—or morning—to last forever, I know Dad will be waking up in an hour to get ready for work and while he trusts my decisions, he may be a little concerned to find me out here at this time of the night—or should I say morning?—with a guy.

"I wish I could, but I need to get some sleep." I frown.

I've had more social interaction in the last twenty-four hours than I have had my entire life. I was finally able to fit-in instead of standing out, and Clay has made me feel things I didn't know were possible. The zest of life that I feel is astounding. I feel like I have opened my eyes to a world of adventure and acceptance, something I have never had before.

"Yeah... yeah, me too." He stands up. "I'll see you tomorrow. You're coming, right?"

I cross my arms. "I'll come under one condition."

"A condition, huh? What's your condition?" he laughs.

I hold out my pinky.

"You have to promise that you will still be my friend tomorrow."

"I promise," he says, and wraps his pinky around mine, and pulls me in for a hug. All it takes is that gentle squeeze for me to begin melting into his arms.

"You have to make me a promise now." He rests his chin on my head.

I pull back and look up at him. "What kind of promise would you want from me?"

"Promise me that you won't change for anyone."

"I... I'm not," I insist, but also wonder if it's the truth.

"Just promise." He stares deep into my eyes and holds out his pinky.

I take it into mine. "I promise."

"Good. Now go get some sleep, you little rebel." We both laugh.

I feel so safe and content in his arms and I don't want to let go. Clay holds me for what feels like minutes, and what I sense inside of myself scares me a little bit.

I sneak in the side door. I shut it behind me, lean my back up against it, then let out a gasp and whisper: *Best night ever.*

Chapter Eight

I wake up to the very loud and obnoxious sound of my aunt's voice yelling from the bottom of the steps: "*Rebecca Ann!*"

I lift my chin to look over at Becca—still asleep on the floor—and the thumping in my head is too much to handle. I pull the pillow over my face and hope she will just get up.

Aunt Meg comes busting through the door. "Wake up, Becca, we have to get going." Her orders are still just as loud and stern, but at least they aren't echoing through my brain this time.

I keep the pillow pressed tightly over my head in hopes of avoiding any conversations about last night.

"I'm coming, MOM!" Becca heaves a sigh and I think she is surely up now.

I peek out just enough to thank them for coming and say goodbye. Aunt Meg leans down and kisses my forehead.

"You may want to shower and brush your teeth before your dad gets home from work," she whispers, flashes me a half-smile, and pulls the blankets up on me.

She knows I drank. I feel a flood of regrets, because my aunt has always looked at me as the perfect child. I pull the pillow back over my head in defeat as they leave.

Soon after, Amber lets me know that her mom is coming to pick her up. I apologize again for my actions last night and she tells me not to worry about it. But I do, of course. Worrying for my people is as much a part of me as an arm or leg; I don't have a choice.

The majority of my morning, after I rinse my mouth at least five times and shower, is spent lying in bed writing. Aunt Meg was bad enough; if Dad finds out I drank last night, he will be so disappointed. Lily and Rose, meanwhile, are packing for a weeks-long trip to LA where they'll visit a friend from high school. They plan to leave tomorrow afternoon—after begging me to go with them and me constantly declining, they gave up asking.

I finally manage to pull myself out of bed to face the day.

"Fun night?" Rose asks as she flips through channels on the T.V.

"Something like that." I put my hand to my head, and I plop down beside her.

We start talking about dinner and the Kellers' pool party. I'm still unsure about the latter, even though I imagine it will be laidback and alcohol-free, since Mr. and Mrs. Keller will be there. The mayor would never allow underage drinking at his home.

After a stint of lounging to recover, I throw my hair up in a ponytail, settle on wearing a simple pink sundress with my white graduation sandals, and leave off the makeup today. I am back to being plain Iris. Inside, though, I feel like I have changed, like a fresh leaf that has sprung from a tree. The same branch but with a polished new feature. Last night opened my eyes to a whole world of possibilities. Not a world of drinking and late-night swimming, but a world of being carefree and enjoying life a little bit.

I grab my notebook and pencil, and stick them into my bag with my swimsuit and towel. Hopefully I don't find myself in a corner on a lounge chair writing, but if this goes south and I'm not feeling the swimming thing, I'll need to do something to pass time.

Lily grabs a desert she prepared and I slump down into the backseat of her car, hoping her driving skills have improved so I don't show up with a nice shiner on my forehead. Dad drives separately in his truck so we can stay for the party.

When we arrive for dinner, I am feeling a little nervous. Clay said he wouldn't ignore me, but after last night, I hope there isn't any residual tension or awkwardness. (He did see me in my bra, after all.)

We are greeted at the door by Mrs. Keller. She wraps her arms around me and her hug makes me think of my mom. Mrs. Keller is such a kind and sweet lady, and the scent of her vanilla body spray gives me a feeling of comfort. When Mom passed away, she would check in on us often and bring dinner over for my dad. She always made me feel at peace.

I've never been inside the Kellers' place, and it's like something out of a *Home and Garden* magazine. Mrs. Keller has decorated it beautifully with a rustic charm. Perfect flowers blink open around the whole house, and a large swing sits in the front porch. Everything is put tidily in its place and it smells of apples and cinnamon.

We are taken out back to the patio, and spotting the poolside grill, I feel relief. I originally imagined that we'd be having a sit-down dinner; the thought of unwanted glances from everyone at the table made me tense. Instead, Mr. Keller is standing over the grill, donning a red apron that reads *Grill Master*.

We all sit down at the patio table. Clay still isn't here. I keep looking around, waiting for him to join us.

Everyone is discussing the Fourth of July festival that is quickly approaching when he finally emerges.

"Glad you could join us," Mr. Keller says, sounding annoyed. "Clay had a late night last night."

I hold my head down to hide the small smile parting my lips. Clay grabs a burger from the middle of the table without sitting.

"Iris did, too," Dad says. My eyes widen and snap up.

Everyone is looking back and forth from me to Clay. They can't possibly know that we were together. My face feels hot and I pray that someone will say something and change the subject.

"The burgers are really good, Mr. Keller," Lily chimes in. *Thank you, Lily.*

Clay pulls a chair up directly across from me, and throughout dinner, we make random eye contact and share a few smiles, all while laughing at my dad's ridiculous farm jokes. Dad has always had a way of entertaining people and getting along with every person he meets. It doesn't matter if they are rich or poor—he sees everyone as an equal and believes success isn't measured by materialistic belongings or money. One of the many things I admire about him.

After dinner, my sisters and I help Mrs. Keller clean up and wash dishes. I imagined she didn't get much help from her sons when it came to household chores, but I'm proved wrong when Clay comes in, carrying the grilling utensils and returning again with the food platters. He brushes against me when he places them in the sink and I feel as though it was intentional.

Some of the boys' friends start arriving for the pool party and join the guys out back. After about a half-hour, Dad takes off, leaving me and my sisters. Clay still hasn't talked to me, but he really hasn't said much to anyone. He seems sort of down today—though that may be from lack of sleep.

The girls summon me into the pool house to change. I grip my bag with both hands and wish that I hadn't given in to their nagging about this stupid swimsuit. Maybe I can make an escape and just hide in a corner chair somewhere.

"Oh, no, you don't." Rose pulls me back as I try to sneak away. "Have some fun and let loose," she says. I feel like I did enough of that last night.

I give in once again, anyway, and put on the swimsuit, tugging my dress back over it until I decide to get in the water—*if* I decide to, at all. The pool area is getting pretty full now and Mr. Keller is a lighting the fire pit outside the gate. I find myself a nice, comfortable lounge chair and sit back to read *Little Women* while everyone else interacts. I'm probably setting myself up for humiliation by reading another book during a social gathering, but I've never been one to try and impress.

The music is loud and the guests all seem to be having a good time. I'm starting to enjoy myself a little bit, too, though—as you know well by now—I'm more of a sit-back-and-watch kind of gal.

"Long time, no see." Clay takes a seat next to me.

I close my book and look over at him. "Yeah, long time," I chuckle and feel the faintest edge of a blush.

"You see what I'm doing here?" He points to me and then himself.

"What exactly *are* you doing?"

"I'm keeping my promise. I'm a man of my word. Always remember that." He laughs, and—feeling flirtatious—I toss him a grin.

"I'll need a little more convincing... but I see that you're trying, so I'll give you that."

Clay tugs my hand in response. "Come in the water. It feels nice."

"I... ugh, I don't know," I stutter, standing, and look around at all of these people.

"I'll go with you." His persuasion is a sexy smile he's been giving me a lot lately.

How can I say no to that? I pull my dress up over my head, revealing my new bikini while at the same time trying to cover myself with my arms. My pale skin confirms that certain parts of my body have never seen sunlight.

"Wow," Clay says, looking me up and down and stopping at my breasts, suddenly making me feel very exposed. "I like your... um, swimsuit."

Clay's reaction patches my lack of self-confidence slightly, and I can't help but smile a little. He takes my hand and leads me to the pool. The water is a bit chilly, but the sun beaming down warms my bare skin. Clay gives me a splash before I can get used to the temperature and teases up goosebumps; laughing in apology, he rubs my arms with both of his hands.

I look around to see if anyone notices our game, worrying they might get the wrong idea, and I spot Luke glaring at us. I don't know why he gets so uneasy any time Clay and I interact; he always has. It feels almost like he doesn't want his brother to be my friend. Maybe that's why Clay always pushes me away when he's near.

Despite Luke's nasty look, I am starting to enjoy myself a little. The twins and I are throwing a big beach ball back and forth when I hear something familiar.

My heart sinks into my chest, burning me from the inside out. I can't tell if it's fury or embarrassment.

"—and then Clay leaned over and put his strong hands around my waist, pulled me into an embrace, and kissed me with those soft lips. His bare skin touching mine as he slid his hand up my shirt—" It's Luke's voice.

His reading is loud enough for the people next to us to hear. Thankfully, it's not everyone, but Clay most definitely heard it all. I stand frozen in the water. I look over at Clay, and he is frozen, as well. He looks just as embarrassed as I am.

It's not real, I want to tell him. If I could make my lips move, I might have said so. I might have called Luke a liar and sworn up-and-down he was just doing it to harass me, that he made it all up. But he didn't. They're my words, and they're terribly, blisteringly real.

"Give it up for Iris Everly and her amazing writing skills." Luke starts clapping.

I rush out of the pool and over to him. I rip my book out of his cold-blooded hand and slap him across the face. He looks shocked, but it doesn't wipe the humor or the malice off. Luke rubs his hand across his cheek and starts laughing. I grab my bag and my dress and make a run for the exit, leaving behind any dignity that I had left.

It's a long walk to my house, but I don't care. I need this time to collect my thoughts.

Tears are dropping down my face and the humiliation that fills my heart and my soul is unbearable. I want to hide away and shut out the world. No one has ever read anything inside this book that I am clutching tightly against my chest. Everyone is going to think that what Luke read was a journal of past events and that's not what this is.

I keep walking without a destination in mind and find myself at our old barn on Mr. Radley's farm. I used to come here to hide away as a child. I sink myself down into the hay in an empty stall and begin to sob uncontrollably. I feel numb and unsure of what to do. I should try and explain this to Clay, but he won't want to hear it; he's probably furious with me.

The friendship that we'd only now started building back up has been destroyed by Luke Keller.

Chapter Nine

After sitting in the barn for what feels like hours, I wipe my tears and decide to face reality. I go home.

Dad is asleep on the couch. That man works himself ragged. I creep up to my bedroom so I don't wake him, and throw myself onto my bed. I can just hear Lily and Rose talking down the hall.

"I got this," Rose says to Lily as she opens my door.

I am lying flat on my stomach, facing the window, and I feel another tear fall from my cheek. They just keep coming now, and I have no control over it. Rose sits down at the bottom of my bed. She hovers there quietly, waiting to see if I want to talk.

"I wanna get a degree in Creative Writing, maybe teach it someday," I tell her.

"What?"

Everyone knows I write all the time, but no one knows what I am writing. They probably all assumed it was my diary from when I was eight. No one has asked, and I have never shared.

"You asked me if I had dreams or if I wanted to stay here like Mom. I want to be a writer," I tell her again.

"Iris, if this is about what..."

I lift my head and I cut her off. "This isn't about what happened. This is me telling you that I do have dreams and that I don't want to be stuck like this forever."

"Then write. I know you have a talent. I've read your school essays and hell, you've even wrote them for me." She laughs.

I sit up cross-legged and brave a smile while playing with the strings in my afghan.

"Don't let Luke stop you from doing what you love. He's an asshole and I told him so. What he did today was inexcusable."

"I don't want to stay here, Rose. I want to go to college and get a degree. I wanna spread my wings and see where I land."

"Then what's stopping you?" She wipes a tear from my cheek.

"Dad." I crumble again. Rose wraps her arms around me while I weep. "I can't leave him all alone. Everyone always leaves him."

"Iris Everly, you get one life to live. Dad wants you to live it—for you." She pokes her finger into my chest. "Lily and I struggled with leaving, too. You know that, but you were the one who told us that we need to take care of ourselves before we can take care of anyone else, and you were right."

"I did say that, didn't I? I guess that's because I always planned to be here."

Rose gets off the bed and walks over to my vanity, and picks up the letter from Washington State. She hands it out to me. "Open it."

I shake my head. "Rose, I have 4.0 and a four-year scholarship. I know I got in," I chuckle. "I don't want to go to Washington State."

She blinks at me, baffled. “Why not?”

I get more serious now. "I've never wanted to go there. I just applied because I felt like I needed to apply somewhere, considering I graduated at the top of my class. A big university is not only intimidating to me; I also feel like I would lose track of myself. I want to go with you and Lily," I tell her. Bellevue isn't exactly close, but WSU is twice the distance.

"Then come with us." She hugs me. "I'll be right back." With that, my sister springs up and rushes out of my room.

Rose returns with her laptop. She sits on my bed and opens it up, takes a minute to navigate to whatever she’s looking for, then turns it to me and places it in my lap.

"Apply at Bellevue. Even if you aren't one-hundred percent sure yet, at least get the admissions stuff done so that when the time comes, you are prepared, whether you go or not."

I put my hands on the laptop and let out a sigh. I can't believe I'm even doing this. I was so set on staying home and just working at the diner and maybe taking an online course or something—not this. The tilt towards my future feels immense. "Where would I stay?" I ask her.

"With us, in the resident halls. You probably won't actually be in the same apartment because they are limited to two people, but you would get a roommate."

I nod in agreement, and even though I'm not convinced that I am ready for all of this, I fill out the admissions paperwork online. She's right. *I have nothing to lose by applying,* I remind myself.

"Thank you, Rose." I smile.

"You're welcome. And Iris, remember what I said: Don't let Luke get to you. Karma is a bitch and he will get his."

I had forgotten all about what happened today until she mentioned it. My stomach drops and my heart sinks again. I don't know how I will ever be able to face anyone in that family.

Morning is quiet at the house. The girls are preparing to leave for LA, and Dad had to go to the farm to talk to Mr. Radley, so we decide to skip church. I need to be at the diner in an hour. In the meantime, I make a quick lunch for us all, and am putting Dad's food in the refrigerator when the phone rings.

"Hello," I answer.

"Iris, it's Clay. I was wondering if you could meet me at the lake?"

I'm silent for a minute as I try come out of this shock. Clay has never called me. Not ever.

"I have to go to work," I respond.

There is a sadness in his voice. "Can you meet me after work?"

"Sure, OK. I'll see you a little after five."

"See ya." He hangs up.

Part of me is happy Clay is reaching out—but the other part of me fears that he's only doing it to tell me we can't be friends anymore. I'm nervous about talking to him. I wipe my damp palms on my apron and take a few deep breaths to slow my rapid heart rate. I'm thankful for the time that I have to mentally prepare myself to see him but I can't let it interfere with work.

My shift goes by insanely slow. The diner is dead except for an elderly couple and they are only my third table today; needless to say, my tips won't be anything to brag about. I'm supposed to be picking up a couple extra shifts starting next week, but my mind wanders to the possibilities of a new job with better pay if I move to Bellevue. I also like the idea of being only twenty minutes away from my cousin and aunt; Becca, too, has mentioned going to Bellevue Community College. I never paid much attention before, because anytime anyone would talk about college, I'd shut down. I wonder if I could just stay with Aunt Meg. *If I could—*

I shake these spiraling thoughts from my head, because the more I think about it, the more I want to go—but the more I lament the thought of Dad being here all alone, too.

Eventually, my dead shift ends, and I'm already getting worked up again. My palms are sweating and my heart is racing. I arrive at the lake a few minutes early; Clay isn't here yet, so I sit in my car and reread the line of my notebook Luke shared with everyone yesterday. I sure am glad he didn't keep going, because that would have really been a page-turner.

Before I can dismay too much over the what-if, Clay pulls up; I stuff my notebook under my seat, and get out.

Clay is looking as appealing as ever in a black T-shirt, gym shorts, and tennis shoes. His dark hair really brings out the sea green eyes of his that always draw me in. I comb my fingers through my ponytail, knowing that I look terrible. A glance down makes me realize I'm still wearing my waitressing apron, so I pull it off and throw it in the car.

"Thanks for coming," Clay says as he leans up against the hood of my car.

"Clay... I'm so—"

He holds his hand up. "'Me first."

Then, on a gasp of air: "Luke should have never invaded your privacy like that. I can't imagine how that felt. I know how I felt but that's besides the point. He told me that after he stopped reading out loud, he read the next couple lines to himself, and it talked about us sleeping together." He looks down long enough to shake his head, then back, and disappointment is brimming in his eyes. "Did you tell people that we slept together, Iris?"

"What?! No!" I yell. "Clay, you don't understand. That wasn't writing about my experiences."

"What the hell was it then, Iris?" I usually love the way he says my name, but this time there is so much ill feeling in his voice.

I walk over to my car and grab my notebook and the slam it into his chest. "It's this. Read it."

He opens the book and reads the first page out loud. "*Destined to Be*."

"It's a book I've been writing, Clay." I feel a rush of embarrassment and worry he will not be very understanding about this, so I give it my best shot, and put myself out there. "It's a book about our lives. About growing up together and our first kiss. It's all factual until I ran out of stuff to write because we drifted apart. I began to write the things I wished for... for us." I turn my whole body away from him and look at the lake, hoping there is a glimmer of acceptance behind me.

"I had no idea. Why didn't you tell me? We spent hours talking the other night—you could have mentioned it."

"Yeah, right. I was just going to open up and tell you that I've been writing a book about a love that doesn't exist between us." Tears surge again. I'm so tired of crying in front of people, but I've restrained my inner self so long, I can't help it.

"Sure, something, anything that could have prepared me." He turns me around.

"Well, I'm sorry, it's not like I knew your dickhead brother would read it to the world."

Clay wipes a finger under my eyes to stop my tears from falling—and, just when I think I've lost him forever, his lips touch mine.

This kiss is different than the others—each one is—but this one is passionate and deep and my hormones take control of my body and I can't let go. I wrap my arms around his neck as he wraps his around my waist and then brings both hands up to my face, cupping my cheeks in his palms.

"I'm not mad at you," he whispers.

Unsure what any of this means, I just go with it. I know that Clay is probably not ready to give all of his heart to me—and I don't feel like I am ready, either—but I want to enjoy getting there.

We stand in from of my car, silent for a couple minutes, and Clay just holds me in his arms. I wasn't expecting any of this coming here today. Hell, I wasn't ever expecting any of this, but there is a part of me that longed for it. I longed to feel his touch and his breath on my skin. It took us a long time— our whole lives—to get to this point, and now that we're here, I don't want to lose it. I have to know what he is feeling.

"What now?" I pull away and look into his eyes.

He smiles. "I want to read your book."

As much as I want Clay to know how I feel and as much as I want him to allow me to feel more, I'm not ready to be that vulnerable yet.

"It's not finished." I smile back, though, still holding my arms around him.

"Let me read what you have and then we can create the end together." He kisses the tip of my nose.

I'm pretty sure I'm blushing at this point, and euphoria has taken over my body. It's terrifying but exciting.

"How about this? I will let you read one chapter every day that you spend with me. It's a win-win, really. You get what you want and I get what I want."

"Deal. Now hand it over." He holds his palm out, and I place the book inside.

Clay heads for the tree, gesturing for me to come with him. He settles down to rest his back against it, and I sit between his legs while he holds the notebook out in front of us. The beginning is easy; these first couple pages just talk about my early childhood, mentioning my first-grade teacher and a friend of mine that transferred schools and the sadness I felt. It isn't very exciting material, and I fear he's probably bored already. But every once in a while, he leans down and kisses my cheek while he reads, and it sends electricity through my veins.

"Ahhh, ahhh! That's enough." I take the book from him and close it as he approaches *Chapter Two*.

"I like seeing what you thought and felt as a child." He wraps his arms around me and rests his chin on my head. "I can't wait to read what you feel in the present."

"I wish I knew what you felt," I tell him, but then I second-guess myself, and I ponder if I really want to know. I don't want to ruin this.

"I could show you."

His pulls me towards him and I straddle his legs as he puts his hands on my cheeks and my mouth meets his. I could get used to this, but—

"I want to know how you *really* feel. What is all this?" I ask him, once again unsure, but I need to know what I'm getting myself into. My heart can't handle another loss. I should say that, but I don't. Instead, I calm my butterflies, and try, "I don't want to misinterpret your actions as something more than what they are."

"I feel like I have known you my whole life. But I want to know more." He twirls my hair around his fingers.

"I feel the same. But what about Luke?"

"You—we—don't have to worry about him anymore," Clay assures me, though I'm left unaware of precisely what that means.

I don't even want to think about Luke in this moment. Even though Clay understands now, I am furious about the invasion of my private belongings, and my thoughts. I know that everyone else probably thinks I have this psychotic obsession with Clay. It shouldn't matter what everyone else thinks, but I have to face these people in our small town. If Clay continues to turn a blind eye to me every time we're around his friends and family, then I won't be able to continue this. I refuse to be his secret *friend*—I deserve more than that.

"Let's just take this one day... one chapter," he corrects himself, "at a time."

I nod. Everything has happened so fast. Even though my crush started as a child, I never imagined that Clay would have feelings for me. I wonder how long he's felt any kind of emotion towards me. Someday I will get answers, but right now, I'll do what he suggests. *One day at a time.*

We stay under the tree and talk for a while. Time seems to go so quickly when we're together; I lose track of it. Clay has a way of making me forget the outside world and it's like we are the only ones who exist. He tells me about his new internship and his job duties and I tell him about my new shifts at the diner.

"I don't understand why you would want to stay in this town and not go away to school," he says as he pulls me up off the ground.

"It's more of a need than I want." I decide not to tell him about Bellevue yet because I'm still unsure how serious I am about attending. "When you're done with school, do you plan to move back?" I wonder as we walk over to the lakeside.

He puts his arms around me from behind as we both stare into the abyss of the lake. "Probably not. I've always wanted out. The small-town bullshit gets old after a while."

"That's true, but I love our town. I'm not pleased with all the drama, but I've always done a good job staying away from it... until Luke." I let out a whimper.

"Eh, that'll all blow over and everyone will find something else to talk about. Like Mr. Sanford's affair with the lady at the post office," he laughs.

"No way!"

The sun starts to set as we laugh together. I have to get home to make dinner for Dad, so we say our goodbyes and agree to meet here tomorrow night to watch the sunset. I'm already looking forward to it.

As we walk back to our vehicles, I notice a nice and new white SUV parked facing towards us. Clay freezes in his tracks.

Our fingers are intertwined for only a moment longer—he lets go abruptly when Lexi steps out of the car.

Chapter Ten

"I thought I might find you here." She stands right in front of us with her arms crossed over her chest, all blonde hair and rolling eyes.

Lexi is beautiful on the outside but unpleasant on the inside. She has always had a way of making me feel inadequate. Her long tan legs meet her ripped black shorts, and her red bra blares through a cropped white T-shirt, matching a perfect manicure. I look down at my bare nails and my dirty feet.

"How did you know I was here?" Clay asks as he hits a button on his keys to unlock his truck.

"Oh, I don't know, maybe because you always used to bring *me* here." She shrugs her shoulders.

The idea that Clay used to bring Lexi here—to my spot—is unsettling. I did see them here once last summer when I was walking, but I turned around and went to the left side of the lake instead before they noticed.

"What's this all about?" She points her finger back and forth between Clay and me.

"What I do is none of your damn business," he retorts.

I begin to feel like maybe I should leave, but for the sake of moving forward with Clay, I need to know what's happening between these two, once and for all.

"That's not the feeling that I got last night."

Last night? What the hell? I hope he didn't sleep with her. My heart plummets—*not again*—and I begin to feel like I've been played. His words were so genuine and his touch was so soft, it felt real to me, but why would he say and do all of these things if he's still sleeping with Lexi?

"Weren't you leaving?" Lexi glares at me and her words sting.

I look over at Clay one last time, hoping against hope he'll stand up for me. But apparently that's asking too much—and when he doesn't, I begin to walk away.

"I'll call you later," I hear him say from behind me.

"Don't bother," I shoot back without turning around.

I get in my car, and standing there with Lexi, Clay doesn't even look at me. Here we go—back to square one. Just when I thought we may have moved forward and built something, he crushes my heart and pulls me down.

This time I don't cry. I don't feel like I have it in me right now.

I wake up the next morning and try to push the thoughts of Clay out of my head. Dad is at work and then has to go take care of something at the bank. He's been going there a lot lately; I hope everything is OK and we aren't on the verge of losing the house, or anything. But when I bring it up, he assures me that everything is fine. *It's just business,* he says. That's all.

After doing some chores and getting dressed, I call Amber to see if she wants to come with me to get a cell phone and then for a manicure and pedicure. I've never had my nails professionally done, but I really liked the way it looked on Lexi. Although she has given me reason to believe that her heart is ugly—she has always looked down on those around her, and treated them as if they just suck from the air she breathes—she is beautiful on the outside.

When we walk into the mall to make for the cell phone stand, I notice a cute maroon-colored, high-neck tank top, paired with some cut off white shorts in a window that catch my eye. It's not something I would usually wear, but my taste is changing rapidly, and I realize I ought to get up-to-speed on the latest styles. After purchasing a couple of outfits and getting my phone all set up, we get our nails done, and I feel like a new person. It's amazing how pampering yourself can really take your mind off things. I need more change. I want to show Clay what he's missing, so I do something drastic that I swore I would never do, and I get highlights. My self-esteem still isn't where it should be, but even I admit I look pretty damn good.

After filling up my gas tank, I realize I am officially broke again, so I give some more thought to college and a job in the city. It sounds more and more promising each day, but I'm still not convinced I'm ready for it.

Dad compliments my new hair—after advising me that I don't need to change my appearance and that he sees me as a natural beauty—although he doesn't understand the struggles of trying to fit in when you've always stood out. We spend the evening watching movies, and Clay never calls. So much for watching the sunset together. I decide to add Facebook to my phone while I'm lying on the couch, and after an hour, I finally have a page. I add a few friends, including my sisters, and they post jokes about me finally joining the Facebook world. I take a selfie of the new me and make it my profile picture. Not even an hour later, I receive a notification of a friend request from Clay—I ignore it.

It's one o'clock in the morning when I hear an awful *beep*. Thinking the smoke detector is going off, I jump out of bed only to realize it's the default alert chime on my phone.

I pick it up and see a message from Clay.

You broke your promise, it reads.

I text back: *What are you talking about?*

Your pinky promise to me. You said you wouldn't change yourself.

What does it matter to you?

I liked your hair the way it was before.

I didn't change it for you, I changed it for myself, I insist, my unpracticed fingers flying as fast as I can make them. *Besides, you broke your promise to me.*

No, I didn't. You will always be my friend.

You have an awful way of showing it. Thanks for ditching me yesterday and blowing me off tonight.

I didn't ditch you. You were leaving anyway and then you told me not to bother calling. What are you upset about?

If you really have to ask then I have nothing more to say to you.

I put my phone down and feel the anger rising in me. This guy is clueless; I have no idea how he held a relationship with Lexi as long as he did. Maybe they both treat each other like dirt, but I won't allow anyone to treat me that way—that's not any kind of relationship that I want.

There's that awful beep again. I monkey with my settings and try to change it, but finally just turn the volume down. Then I give in to my heart and read the message.

Is this about Lexi? I told you we are done.

I think you and I have a different definition of the word done.

She's still a friend.

Is this what he does to his friends? I wonder how many other girls he toys with like this.

His next message is like a cup of cold water to the face:

I just want to make sure that I didn't give you any mixed signals. I'm not really looking for a relationship with you. I just figured we could get to know each other better.

And there it is. The clarification I was looking for. I can't believe that part of me thought we could be more. I feel used and led-on and it hurts deeply. Why would I ever think he wanted me as a girlfriend? I feel stupid and humiliated. Two feelings that I know all too well.

Goodnight, Clay.

I set my phone down and ignore the vibrations it keeps making. I can't even begin to try and shut that damn thing off.

Chapter Eleven

After a restless night of tossing and turning, I ended up stuffing the phone under a blanket on the floor and sticking ear plugs in my ears.

One day, I'll learn how to work it properly. Today, I grab the wretched thing and go downstairs to have breakfast. I push the button to take me to the main screen and it is flooded with messages from Clay.

My jaw drops open. There are at least fifteen messages from him. *He must have been drinking,* I think to myself as I read through them.

Why are you so mad?

Please answer me.

Iris, are you still there?

I said I was sorry.

Did you get your cell phone? What's your number?

Can I call you?

Iris?

Get your ass out of bed and answer me.

That's it, I'm coming over.

What?! Did he come over? I keep reading.

Come down and talk to me.

I know you hear the sticks on your window.

He didn't! I had the earplugs in; I didn't even know. I wonder how long he was out there. What kind of *friend* does this kind of thing?

The messages go on:

Iris, I'm sorry. Will you please come talk to me?

I miss you. You feel so close but so far away.

There are things you don't understand about me, about my life. I care a lot about you and I don't mean to lead you on or give you mixed signals but when I am with you I lose control and I feel things that I shouldn't be feeling.

Are you reading any of this?

I guess I'll leave you alone. You don't want me anyways, Iris, you are too good for me. You deserve to be with someone who can give you their whole heart. I can only give you part of it.

I was OK with part of it. I just want to be respected. I want him to value our friendship and not push me away. I sit back and tears roll down my cheeks onto my freshly-pressed screen protector. I feel this constant push and pull from Clay. He pushes me away and then he pulls me back in—and worst of all, I allow it.

My fingers move as if with a mind of their own.

I didn't know you came.

Without thinking, I hit *send.* Apparently, you can erase messages or add to them even after you send them. I am so illiterate when it comes to technology. Maybe I do need to get out more. I laugh at myself a little. Let's try that again.

What I meant to say, I type, is I didn't know you came over and if I had known I would have come down to talk to you.

He responds immediately: *Headed to my internship. Meet me at 3 at the lake?*

See you then, I agree. And add, for measure: *Good luck.*

The day drags on, and I head down to the lake a little early to write before Clay comes. I decide to walk, since it's a beautiful day. The campground on the way is filling up and loud music blasts from a campsite near the road.

There are a couple of guys hooting and hollering but I walk faster, pretending I don't hear them.

I lay down a blanket and lean against the tree and begin writing. After a few minutes, I notice Clay's truck headed down the path. I continue to write so that my knowledge of his arrival isn't overly obvious.

"Whatcha writing? He plops down beside me.

"Wouldn't you like to know?' I grimace. "Care to fill me in on what happened last night?"

"It looks like rain is coming; let's get out of here." He stands and reaches for my hand.

I ignore his offer to help me up and stand on my own. "OK, then. I guess I'll see you later." I give him and eye roll, feeling like this was a complete waste of time.

"No, no, Iris..." He takes a hold of my hand, stopping me. "I meant let's both get out of here. Come to my house with me. My parents are in New York for some convention."

"Can you just drive me home?" I suddenly don't feel like talking much tonight. Maybe I'm just getting annoyed with this back-and-forth.

"Home? I thought we were gonna talk," he says with a sadness in his voice.

I cross my arms. "Then let's talk."

"Can we sit in my truck?"

I walk over to it, open the passenger door, and get in without saying anything. Clay proceeds to get in the driver's side.

His hands are on the steering wheel and he sits silently for a moment, looking straight ahead. "Are you mad at me?"

"I'm not mad," I tell him. "I'm just confused and a little agitated."

"I get it." He shakes his head.

I feel like this conversation is going nowhere and I'm not sure if I have the courage or energy to dig into it more.

"Iris." he turns towards me. "I know that I haven't made much sense lately and I get why you are confused. I just need you to trust me." He closes his eyes, rubbing his fingers over his temple.

"Honestly, Clay, I don't know why I need to trust you. I don't know what you are to me; I don't even know if I can call you a friend. You kiss me and then you ignore me, you call me and then blow me off. It's getting old." I turn my head and look out the window, surprised the words came out of my mouth and fearing his response.

"Of course we're friends. We have been our whole lives," he says.

I tilt my head toward him with a little eye roll and half-smile. "Come on, Clay. We have known each other for a long time, but can you honestly say that we were friends?" I shake my head. We merely had moments of friendship. We played together when it was convenient for him; we kissed when no one was looking. I was there for him when he needed me but he wasn't there when I needed him.

"Where were you when my mom was sick?"

I can't believe I just said that. Clay's eyes widen at the shock of my question and I can tell he is searching for an explanation.

"I was... I was around," he stutters.

"Around? A friend would have been there with me. You didn't even talk to me at the funeral." I feel myself getting angry and I wish I hadn't brought this up.

Clay rests his head on the steering wheel. "You're right, I should have made more of an effort." He doesn't lift his head.

"I'm sorry, Clay. I shouldn't have said anything."

"No, you should have. I haven't been a good friend. Hell, I haven't been a good person." He looks at me and I can see pain in his eyes. I want more than anything to take that pain away.

"You are a good person," I tell him. I know he is; he just wears a mask to try and impress everyone. I've seen him without it and there is a good man underneath.

"I'm not." He shakes his head. "I screwed up bad at school. I got in a big fight while I was wasted and almost got kicked out. I'm on my last straw with my dad. He told me that if I mess up one more time, he isn't funding my tuition anymore. But that's petty compared to the way I've made you feel. Not just today, but your whole life." He grabs my hand. "Iris, I care about you a lot and I don't mean to hurt you."

"I had no idea. Not that you cared about me—well, that, too—but the school stuff." I put my hand over his and feel like I'm getting sucked back in.

"Yeah, it was pretty bad so I've been trying hard not to disappoint him again. So far it hasn't worked." He shrugs his shoulders. "But that's not what we came to talk about. I want to talk about us."

"Clay, I forgive you. We don't need to hash it out. From this point forward, just please have a little more respect for me and consider my feelings when we are around each other." I look into his eyes and as much as I want to just kiss him, I'm refusing to tonight. He needs to show me that it means something.

"I will. I promise," he says.

I want to believe him, but I'm going to let him prove it first.

"Could you drive me home? I'm a little nervous to walk tonight."

"You don't even have to ask. I wasn't gonna let you walk, anyways. I was hoping maybe you'd come over and hang out, though. What do you say?"

As much as I want to, I really just need to go home and think about all of this—and maybe not giving into him so much will help with this respect thing. "I think we should quit while we are ahead." I pause, and extend my hand. "Friends?"

He gives me a strange look like I did something wrong. "Yes, we are friends, but..." He trails off.

"Good, it's settled." Even though he didn't shake my hand.

We drive back to my house in silence, where I simply thank him and say goodbye with a smile. He seems rather annoyed, but he needs to learn that he can't always get what he wants. I refuse to be at his beck and call.

Walking up to my house, my phone beeps. There's a message already waiting.

You owe me a chapter.

I laugh to myself. He's right: I do.

Chapter Twelve

The next morning is quiet around the house. Dad is already at work and the girls are in LA. I should be used to the silence, but lately, it feels so lonely. I feel the need to get out and do something, so I decide to take a chance and message Clay.

What are you doing today?

He doesn't respond right away, so I tuck my phone in a front pocket of my dress and decide to go for a drive into town and get a coffee.

When I walk into the coffee shop, I notice Luke and some of his friends sitting at a table, so I turn to walk out—but when I reach for the door, I hear him.

"Iris, wait," he calls to me, and I am already preparing for the string of insults to my character.

"Luke." I put my hand up. "Not today, please."

At this distance, I notice he has a cut lip and a black eye. He must have really pissed someone off.

"I wanted to apologize. I shouldn't have done what I did." Luke doesn't sound very sincere, but it's probably taken a lot for him to even be civil, let alone apologize.

"Fine, thanks." I walk over to the counter and he follows. His friends are watching us intently.

"I really am. I invaded your privacy and that was wrong."

"You've treated me like dirt my whole life, Luke. I don't expect anything from you. Go on with your life; I'll be just fine." I give him a little shoo with my hand.

"It was all for fun." He isn't exactly helping his case.

"Iced mocha with no whip," I tell Annie, the barista, and hand her my money.

I turn to Luke, rolling my eyes. "I'm so glad that you can have fun at my expense."

Just then my phone beeps, and I pull it out of the pocket of my dress. It's Clay.

I have today off, come over.

Luke catches a glimpse and I feel invaded again.

"Is that Clay?"

"That is none of your business," I stammer, putting my phone back into my pocket and taking my coffee so I can get out of this place before he ruins my day.

He follows me out the door until we are both standing outside. "What's going on with you two?"

"Why do you care?"

"Because he's my brother and he doesn't need anyone messing up his life."

"You think *I* am trying to mess up his life?" I put my hand on my chest and giggle at the ridiculousness of the notion.

"Not you in particular, but girls. After what Lexi did to him, he lost it and started screwing up towards the end of last semester at school—drinking all the time, fighting. I'm just looking out for him."

"Clay and I are just friends. I only want what's best for him. I would never hurt him." Strange times: I wonder why I'm even bothering to tell him any of this, and why he hasn't teased me yet.

"You don't do this to defend *just a friend*." He points to his eye.

I clasp my hand over my mouth. "Clay... did that? But why?"

"The night of the pool party, after everyone left, he went crazy and told me to stay away from you. He broke a bunch of shit and our dad had to pull him off me."

My phone beeps again but I ignore it.

"He must really care about you," Luke says, now sounding sincere. "All the more reason for you to let him down gently."

I shake my head and begin to walk to my car, and this time, he doesn't follow. But he yells instead: "You'll both end up hurt in the end."

Who does this guy think he is, trying to pass judgment and assumptions on me? It's hard to focus on my disgust with Luke, though. I can't believe Clay punched his own brother in my defense. It makes me happier than it should. I don't want to interfere with family, but Luke has been asking for it for a long time, and I'm just glad Clay finally stood up for me.

I get in my car and message him back.

I'm on my way.

Luke spouted a lot of information designed to keep me away from Clay, but on the contrary, knowing makes me want to be with him even more. He told me he cares about me—a lot.

I knock at the front door and Clay greets me with a smile. His parents are still in New York, so I feel a little more at ease knowing that it's just us here. Then I begin to feel a little tense, *because* it is just us here.

Clay is shirtless, revealing his tanned and well-toned body. Sweat is pooling on his forehead and I assume he has been working out. I stand and stare a moment with the door open before I catch myself.

"Um, hi," I spit out.

"Hey, come on in." He gestures. I walk past him clutching my bag, notebook and phone tucked inside. I know that Clay hasn't forgotten he gets to read a couple chapters.

"You can go in there." He points to the living room. "I'm just gonna grab a shirt."

The living room is cozy and the electric fireplace is lit, calming the room. Keller boys' pictures line up on the mantle and a large family portrait hangs over top. Clay has such a charm in his pictures. The lips parting around his smiles make me think of the way they felt touching mine. I long to feel that touch again.

I jump when Clay places a hand on my shoulder. "Sorry," he says and we both start laughing.

We sit on the couch and decide to watch a movie. Clay looks comfortable and laidback in the reclining section of the couch, and I sit tense with my feet on the floor and my hands in my lap. The movie isn't of much interest to me, but just being in Clay's company is enough to keep me satisfied. "Come here," he says and I scoot a little to my left.

"A little further." He pulls me to him by the waist and puts his arm around my neck; I lay my head on his shoulder. "Why are you so tense?"

"I'm not, I'm just watching the movie." I point to the T.V.

He tells me to relax but I'm having a hard time doing so. I know that I need to stop over-thinking everything and just be myself, but it's hard when I feel so bedazzled by him. He must have felt the same way about the movie as I did, because when I look up, his eyes are shut. I can feel his deep breaths and hear the sound of his beating heart. He looks so peaceful and I don't want to wake him, so I stay very still, and next thing I know, I'm drifting to sleep, as well.

Chapter Thirteen

The smell of charred smoke breaks my deep sleep. I rub my eyes and look over, and Clay is no longer on the couch.

I rip off the soft white throw blanket Clay must have put on me, jump off the couch and run into the kitchen, where he's waving an oven mitt back and forth, trying to get the smoke away from the smoke detector. It finally stops.

"What happened?" I shriek, grabbing a pan off the stove and submerging it into a water-filled sink. The embarrassed look on his face is adorable and it's an expression that I will never forget.

"I… umm… tried to cook you dinner."

My heart melts into tiny little pieces. No one has ever done anything like this for me before. It may be burnt and inedible, but he put thought into it just for me.

I pick up a chunk of black meat floating in the water; it appears to be chicken. We both start laughing uncontrollably.

"You did this for me?" I wrap my arms around his neck. This is a side of Clay that I've never seen before and I wasn't sure that it existed.

"Well, I tried." The embarrassed look returns and my heart aches for him. With no thinking or planning, I press my lips into his.

His arms wrap around my waist and the yearning I feel tells me that I may not be able to stop myself. His lips move down to my neck and send chills through my body. Clay picks me up and I twine my legs around him as he carries me to the couch; his lips move back to mine and his teeth tug my bottom lip. He lays me on the couch and the weight of his body feels heavy on mine but in a way that brings pleasure instead of pain. I feel the warmth of his hand climb up my shirt and, unsure what to do, I grasp his shirt and pull it over his head. *'Is this really happening?'* I think to myself.

Nope. I hear the door slam shut and Clay jumps up and fumbles to put his shirt back on. I try to catch my breath before I get up. All I can think in this moment is, *please don't be his parents, please don't be his parents.*

I'm relieved but annoyed when I hear Luke's voice. "What the hell happened in here?"

I stand and he is looking towards the kitchen. The stove is covered in sauce and there is still chicken floating in the sink.

"I'll clean it up," Clay grumbles. I wonder if he is as disappointed as I am.

"What? Are you two playing house now?" Luke looks over at me and his expression is blank.

"Fuck off," Clay shouts. "I told you to stay out of my damn business."

I feel like I ought to go in the kitchen and clean up, but maybe I should just leave. I grab my keys and my bag and start walking to the door. "I should go," I say.

"No, he needs to go." Clay points his finger vigorously at Luke. "Let's just go to my room." He takes my hand and leads me. Luke stands with his head hung low with a combination of guilt and shame as he fidgets with his keys in his hand.

Knowing that we won't be able to pick up where we left off, I just sit on his bed. "I'm sorry," I say softly.

"What are you sorry for?" He sits next to me, taking my hand into his.

"Causing problems with you and Luke." I trace my other finger on this inside of his palm. They are fighting because of me and it hurts to know. I blurt it without thinking: "Maybe I should have just stayed away from you, like he said."

Clay erupts from the bed with anger boiling behind his eyes. "What?" He shouts it, but I know his anger is toward his brother. "Did he tell you to stay away from me?" He stops in front of me.

I can't find the words. Before I do, Clay storms out of his room, slamming the door shut behind him and I know I just made a big mistake. What do I do? What if he punches Luke again? What if Luke punches him? I can't bear the thought of him getting hurt, so I rush out after.

"Clay... Clay, wait," I call, but he doesn't listen. Next thing I know, Clay is slouched over in Luke's face where he sits on the couch.

"I thought I told you to mind your own damn business and to stay away from her." I have never seen Clay this furious before. It terrifies me.

"Clay, stop!" I yell, pulling him by his arm and away from Luke.

"This is between me and him, Iris. It has nothing to do with you." He frees his arm and I beg for him to come back to his room. But his hostility softens when he talks to me. "Please just go in my room while we talk."

"Please, Clay. Come with me." I give him another gentle pull away.

"Everything is fine. I just need to talk to my *brother*." The word is laden with sarcasm.

I decide to go, because he seems less enraged at this point. Maybe they need to just talk this out. I stop in the kitchen, out of their sight, when I hear Clay's quiet, irate voice: "What were you doing talking to her? You think you can pull her away from me like you did with Lexi."

What does Lexi have to do with this? I stand silently and listen.

"It's not like that, Clay. You know I have no interest in Iris."

"Really? You said the same about Lexi," Clay thunders. "Do you think you would have a chance with her if I was out of the picture?"

I'm trying to wrap my brain around this whole conversation. Clay thinks that Luke is interested in me. That's impossible.

Luke has never even been nice to me. If I explain that to Clay, then maybe he will lay off a little bit.

"No!" Luke shouts back. "I don't want Iris. I was just trying to protect you."

"Oh, yeah. Just like you were trying to 'protect' me by fucking my girlfriend when I was away at school?"

My stomach and my jaw drop at the same time. This is so much bigger than I imagined.

I hear a loud thud and hurry into the living room, where Luke is lying in the floor holding his face, and blood is dripping onto the perfect white carpet.

"What did you do?" I grab some paper towels from the kitchen and hurry over to Luke.

"Let's get out of here." Clay snatches his keys from the counter and storms out the front door.

I run out after him. "We can't just leave him like that." I keep trying to grab Clay's shirt but he's walking too fast. "Clay, stop!" I demand and he turns to me. "I'm not going anywhere until you tell me what the hell just happened in there."

"He'll be fine. I just busted his lip back open."

I turn around when I hear the front door slam and Luke is stalking towards his truck. "You stay! I'll go," he concedes, calmly, but there is hurt written all over his face.

I feel for both of them. I know how close I am with my sisters, and the Keller boys have always had that same bond. The idea of something like this happening between the twins and I is unbearable. I can only hope they face and fix what is broken before it's too late and they lose each other forever.

Clay and I go back into the house, and I begin to clean up the mess in the kitchen. "You don't have to do that," he promises, but I insist, and scrub at the pan that once contained my dinner.

I chuckle to myself as I work at it. "I still can't believe you tried to cook for me."

"I *can* cook." He wraps his arms around me and kisses my neck. "I was just too distracted by your snoring."

"I do not snore." I swat at him.

"Oh, you do snore, but that's nothing compared to the drool." He tickles my side and I squirm, trying to get away from him.

"Now I *know* you're lying," I declare, which only inspires Clay to start in on the snoring sounds, and I poke at him until he stops.

We finish cleaning the kitchen and throw some pizza rolls in the oven, setting a timer to avoid any further smoke inhalation. The bloodstains on the carpet have been scrubbed, too, and we assume Luke must have done it before he left. I still cringe at the sight of him lying there. I thought for sure that Clay had broken his nose.

We watch our next movie in Clay's bedroom, just in case Luke returns.

Someday they'll have to have it all out, but I prefer they do it when their parents are home and I'm not here. I don't know if I could handle that again.

Lying in Clay's bed with him feels so natural right now. We have taken such big steps today in the right direction and I'm hoping to get some clarity on what we are very soon. I don't want to rush anything and push him away, especially since his breakup is probably fresh in his mind and heart, but for my own sanity, I need to know if he feels what I feel.

My phone beeps and Clay hands it to me from the night stand. It's an email from the Bellevue admissions office; they've made a decision on my application. Though I expected a much longer wait, I'm pleased with the prompt decision. I'm not too concerned, because I can't imagine they wouldn't accept me, but I still need to see with my own eyes. I have to log into my account and can't seem to figure it out on my phone.

"Can I use your laptop?" I ask.

"Sure, go ahead. I'll go check the pizza rolls."

I open the computer and the background wallpaper is of the football team his senior year. He always looked so good in that uniform. Seeing him in this picture makes me feel like he is so far out of my league. I only went to a couple games, but when I did, it was always to secretly watch him. It feels unreal that I am sitting here in Clay's bedroom and we are making food together. If someone told me this would happen, I would have laughed in their face.

Once I'm logged on, I navigate to my admissions letter, and click the file.

ACCEPTED.

"Yay," I breathe, and clap my hands together.

"Bellevue, huh?" Clay startles me.

"Yeah. I figured I'd apply just in case." I sound casual.

"You seemed pretty excited. I always thought that if you went to school, you wanted to go to State."

"Nah, I don't even know if I'm going to Bellevue. But I'm definitely not going to State. Not that it's a bad school," I add, hoping not to offend him. "I just... I don't want to go to a university. I know I listed it as my future school in the yearbook, but that was all for show. I never really wanted to go there."

"I wish you'd reconsider." He sets down a plate of pizza rolls and I'm hoping that he isn't going to try and convince me like everyone else has. "I don't think I can start a relationship with someone who will be four hours away from me."

Start a relationship? He said it, not me. Is that actually what we are doing? I feel ecstatic at the possibility, and then I remember what he just said. If he can't have a relationship someone that far away, it means I'd have to go to Washington State, because it's just as far from home as it is from Bellevue—and that is out of the question.

Clay lies back on his bed with his arms under his head and stares at the ceiling, deep in thought. I sit on the edge. "Is everything OK?"

"Not really." He leans forward, holding himself up on his elbow. His eyes peer into mine. "What do you want from me?"

I am speechless. I thought I would be the one asking him this question; I wasn't prepared for him to ask me. I don't want to pour my heart out and have him laugh at me. I don't want to be the one misreading things once again.

"I... um. I don't know. What do you want from me?"

"No, I asked you first."

I stand up and turn to the wall, crossing my arms. "Well, to be honest, you already said you just wanted to get to know each other, so I didn't think you wanted anything more than friendship with me."

"I asked what *you* want from me. Not what you think I want from you."

I stand silent for a minute to decide how I want to approach this.

"Fine. I'll put it all out there. You are really putting me in an uncomfortable position here." I turn to face and shake my finger at him. "I'm not saying I want a relationship right now, but it's definitely something that I would consider if I knew the feelings were mutual."

I cover my face with my hands like a child, but I can't bear to look at his expression right now.

"The more time I spend with you, the more I see that I need you in my life. I need more of you. When we are apart, I think of you, and when we are together, I can't keep my hands off you." He pulls my hands away from my face and a sense of relief overcomes me. "Now answer my question, because you keep avoiding it based on what I think." His arms wrap around my lower waist and he rests his head on my stomach.

OK—here goes—for real, this time: "I've had a crush on you since I was eleven years old. When you moved out of your old house, I felt like you took part of me with you. These past couple weeks have been the best of my life and I don't want it to end. What I'm saying is that... all I want is you, all of you, but I'm scared." My face feels hot and I'm starting to shake and I know he can feel it.

He looks up at me with his arms still wrapped around me. "What are you scared of?"

"Falling in love. With you." My heart is racing. I can't believe I just said that. I wish I could take it back. He probably thinks I am an obsessed fool.

"Don't ever be scared to love me." He pulls me down gently on top of him.

If I had ever felt like I had any self-control at all, it's out the window right now. Clay flips me over so that I am lying flat on my back. I lose all sense of modesty as he lifts my dress over my head and presses his lips against the bare skin on my ribcage. I gasp when his lips move to my side and he works his way up to my neck. The warmth of his breath sends an indescribable sensation throughout my whole body. His lips meet mine and I pull his shirt over his head. I begin to unbutton his jeans.

"Are you sure?" he asks, placing his hands on my cheeks and peering into my eyes. I can't speak so I just nod. I've never been so sure of anything in my life. I had hoped that Clay would be my first and the realization that it's actually happening causes my heart to pound in my chest. I shiver at his touch when his hands move to my back as he undoes the clasp of my bra. With his arms wrapped around my body, he rolls me over into my back and continues to take off his shorts. His hands move up my inner thigh as I feel the light touch of his finger.

Clay reaches over to his nightstand and retrieves a condom. I trace my fingertips on his back and dig them deeper when I feel a hint of pain as he pushes himself inside me.

"Are you OK?" He asks while his lips graze my neck and I nod.

The pain is noticeable but it is replaced by the compelling desire for more. I can feel his heart beat on my chest and the sweat on his back. This is so much more than just sex to me; I'm overflowed with an agony of emotions. The sounds that escape me are new and intense and I dig my nails deeper, hoping that I'm not hurting him, but when he lets out a deep moan I know that he likes it. His body drops heavily into mine when we finish and I bury my face between his neck and his shoulder as he kisses the top of my head.

"Are you OK?" he asks again.

"Yes." This time I can speak. I just want to lie in this moment for an eternity. Our souls feel intertwined, and I can only describe this feeling as love. I love this man. Part of me has always known it, but now I am certain. Lying here with him like this is the most intimate moment of my life—even more intimate than losing myself to him—because it's in this moment that I know for sure I am in love.

Yet I can't help but think about what he said about distance, and what it means for a future we might not have.

"What are you thinking?" He lifts his head and looks at me.

"Nothing," I lie, gently, unsure of what to say. "What are you thinking?"

"I'm thinking that you always answer my questions with questions." He kisses my forehead.

"I'm sorry. I'm just not very good at explaining what I'm thinking or how I feel."

"I've noticed. I get it, though. I'm the same way. To be honest, I've been more open with you than I have with anyone." He rolls over onto his back.

"Really?" I prop myself up on my elbow.

"Really."

"What about..." I stop myself. I don't want to bring her name up, especially in this moment.

"Lexi?" he finishes for me. "Nah, Lexi and I were never more than sex and for show. I thought I had feelings for her but they were never deep, so I never shared anything personal with her. We were together because it made sense at the time but we were all wrong for each other." I feel an immense relief as he runs his fingers through my hair. "Now back to you."

"Well, to be honest, I'm thinking that our pizza rolls are cold." We both start laughing.

We get out of bed. I go into the bathroom to clean up and get dressed, and when I'm done, Clay does the same.

"Stay with me tonight." He tucks my hair behind my ear and whispers it from behind me.

"I... I can't," I stutter. "My dad would never be OK with that."

"Tell him you're staying with a friend." He kisses my neck again as a tease and, of course, I give in.

"Stay here," I instruct him as I place my hand on his chest.

I go into Clay's bedroom where it's quiet and suddenly feel very rebellious. I have never done anything like this before. I've never skipped school, cheated, lied about where I was going or staying. Feeling extremely deceitful and nervous, I dial my home number. Dad picks up on the first ring.

"Dad, it's Iris."

"Hi, there. I started to get a little worried," he says. I glance down at my phone and realize it's already seven.

"Sorry about that. I lost track of time watching a movie with Amber. Do you mind if I stay here tonight?" I begin twirling my hair around my finger.

"No, go ahead. I'm gonna go to bed early. Long day at work today. Be safe," he tells me. His kindness makes me feel even guiltier.

"Thanks, Dad. There are leftovers in the fridge. I love you."

"Already had dinner at the diner with a friend. Thanks, honey. I love you."

I let out a long sigh and flop down onto Clay's bed. All of this is just so hard to believe. Everything I've ever wanted is happening, and I feel dazed.

"Did you call?" Clay walks into the room and lies down next to me.

"Yep, good to go." I roll over and face him. I've never stayed with a guy before, so I don't know how this works. "What now?"

"Now we eat." He gets up and reaches his hands out for mine, and pulls me up.

The evening is everything I could have wanted. We lie in bed, vegging out and watching the newest *Transformers* movie—Clay's pick—and then it's my turn. I choose *Sweet Home Alabama*. I'm shocked to learn he's never watched it before; I've seen it at least one hundred times; but I suppose it's probably not a hit movie to a guy. Eventually, the screen goes dark, and I'm feeling pretty tired, but what Clay said has been eating away at me so I decide it's a good time to bring it up.

"Can we talk about what you said earlier?" I ask, though I'm not certain I want to know his response to my next question.

"About what?" He sits up with a serious look on his face.

"You said that you didn't want to start a relationship with someone who was as far away from you as I would be at Bellevue. Did you mean it?"

"I did."

My heart shatters. I can't comprehend why he would allow things to go as far as they did when he knew we wouldn't have a future together. I feel sick, and suddenly, I have to get out of this room.

I get up abruptly and rush out. I'm trying to hold it together because I don't want to cry, but I'm not sure if I can stop myself.

He follows me out of his room. "Hey, what's wrong?" Clay looks at me like he has no idea how much those two simple words hurt me.

"If you knew that we would never be together, then why didn't you stop yourself, or stop me?" Tears pool in my eyes, so I turn away from him.

"Because... I guess I was hoping you would change your mind and come with me to Washington State." He sounds so certain of himself.

"Clay, I'm not going there. I told you that. Nothing you say can change my mind." He turns me around and pulls me into him, stroking my head to calm me.

"What if I told you that I love you." He puts his fingers under my chin and lifts my head up and looks straight into my tear-filled eyes. "I love you," he says again.

"Don't say that. Don't tell me that because you think it's what I need to hear," I say with my face an inch away from his.

"I'm not, I mean it. I've always loved you. From the first time that I kissed you when I was twelve years old. When I walked away, I told myself that I was going to marry you one day."

I can't breathe and I feel my heart is no longer beating. I stand frozen and I repeat what he said over and over in my head. Marriage? He loves me?

"But—" I can't finish because he presses his sweet lips into mine. I can't even think right now. I kiss him back.

"I love you, too," I manage in-between breaths. There is so much I want to say, so much that I need to say.

"Why didn't you ever tell me?" I ask him.

"Because, even though you said that you felt like I always pushed you away, I felt like you always pushed me away. I guess it was a whole lot of miscommunication and then when I moved, we sort of grew apart and went our separate ways. I thought of you all the time, though. But society changed us both. I had just always hoped someday time would bring us back together."

"That's exactly how I've always felt." I lay my head on his shoulder while we sit back down on the couch.

"Now that we made our way back to each other, I don't want to be hours away from you. Long-distance relationships never work, Iris." He sounds so genuine and sincere.

"I know. I hope you aren't upset, but I heard your *conversation* with Luke today."

"I figured you probably did. I don't want you to think that I worry you would ever do that to me. I'm just a little more insecure after that, and I obviously no longer trust my brother."

"I get it. I'll think about State." I look up and smile at him. I'm not sure if I am saying this to please him or because I will consider it, but either way, it puts the subject to rest for now.

"Good. It's settled, then." He pats my leg.

"I said I'd think about it."

"I'm not talking about school; I'm talking about us. If that's what you want?" He runs his fingers through his hair and returns them to my leg.

I place my hand on top of his. "It's what I've always wanted."

Clay grabs me and cradles me in his arms, and I start giggling, and he carries me back to his bedroom to set me down. It's getting late now, and I'm tired, so I change into one of his T-shirts to get into bed. We lie there talking until I can no longer hold my eyes open, and I drift to sleep with my head on his chest.

Waking up to Clay the following morning is heavenly. He has bewitched me, body and soul. I still feel like I am in euphoria, and none of this even seems real. The sun is hidden behind his blackout curtains and I have no idea what time it is; I don't even care, as long as I get home and ready for work before 11:30.

The sound of my stomach growling forces us out of bed. "You sit and relax while I attempt to make you breakfast."

"Err. Maybe I should help you." But he shoos me back to the table.

My head is resting on my hand as I watch the beautiful sight of a man cooking for me. I could get used to this. I'm still in disbelief that Clay pictured me as his bride when he was a kid.

Clay places a plate of scrambled eggs and slightly burnt toast in front of me and I applaud him. It actually tastes good, too.

He takes a phone call in the middle of eating and steps away. I can't make out what he says, but I hear him apologize, and he tells the caller he will see them tomorrow. I can't help but wonder if it was Lexi he was apologizing to.

After breakfast, I realize it's getting late, and I need to get home to shower before work. I give Clay a kiss and hug and eventually peel myself off him to leave.

Chapter Fourteen

The next few days, I feel consumed by Clay. We've spent every day together since our big leap in our relationship. He even took me out to dinner—in public—which was a serious step, considering I was worried he would want to keep this a secret for now. I've kept up my end of our deal and let him read chapters of my book each day, and it's getting to the point where I begin to talk about my feelings for him. He seems to like it, though, which delights me. I haven't been writing much lately because I want to wait and see what changes happen in my real-life romance.

I've always been very afraid of change, because when things change, you risk losing people. I've come to realize that, more often than not, when you welcome change, you take a chance at letting new people in. If I hadn't, I would have never let Clay back into my heart. It's terrifying but exciting and although I fear losing him someday, if I don't take this chance, I will always wonder what could have been.

I've also put more thought into going to Washington State, but cannot convince myself. I truly feel we can make it work long-distance. Clay needs to be reassured that not everyone will betray him—that not everyone is cold-hearted. I feel that he knows; he is just scared.

When my sisters come home from LA one night, I fill them in on my new relationship, and make them swear not to tell Dad just yet. They are skeptical due to the way they have seen him treat me in the past, but I assure them that he has matured a lot. Satisfied, they turn conversation to our upcoming trip to Seattle, where we'll visit Becca so she won't be left alone while Aunt Meg goes out-of-town.

Seattle means I won't see Clay for a couple of days. I make plans to meet him at the lake tonight, and decide it's the perfect time to try the new outfit I bought a couple weeks ago with Amber. I even put on a tiny bit of makeup to feel more confident. And, lastly, I drive instead of walking, since I'm still a little creeped-out by the camp guys who were harassing me. They're long gone now, but the memory still plays in my head.

When I arrive, Clay is lying in the back of his pickup truck on a blanket with the tailgate down. He looks so sexy in black shorts and white cutoff T-shirt. His smile when he first sees me sends a wave of excitement through my veins. I climb into the back of the truck and lie with him.

"So, what are your plans for Seattle?" He takes my hand into his and begins kissing it.

"I'm not really sure yet. I'm hoping for a mellow night in but Becca is unpredictable, so it's hard to say. Apparently, she's been hanging with the wrong crowd and getting into some trouble, so I'd like to avoid her friends, if possible."

"Don't let her drag you down with her. I know how you get when you hang out with her." He sounds serious.

"That was just one time. She stayed with me last summer and I never drank."

"Yeah, but you've changed a lot since then." He looks me up and down as if referencing my clothes and my makeup.

"The way I look on the outside has nothing to do with my morals and the way I feel," I tell him, unsure of where this conversation is going.

He lies back down on his folded arms. "I just don't want you to do anything you'll regret."

I, on the other hand, sit up. "Why would you say that? What do you think I would do?"

"Uh, I don't know. Get drunk, cheat on me," he says with a blank expression on his face.

I hover in shock. How can he just casually say something like that without thinking that it would bother me? How dare he assume that just because Lexi cheated on him, I would do the same?

"I'm not Lexi, and I wish you would stop comparing her actions to mine," I spit without thinking and scoot off the tailgate.

Clay sits up. "I'm not comparing. I just know how girls get when they drink."

"Girls!" I shout, and turn to him.

"I didn't mean it like that; I meant to say people." He gets down beside me.

"I'm not like every other person who has screwed you over and I can't believe you are even talking like this." I pull myself away from him and walk down to the lake. We are having our first argument as a couple, and I don't like it at all, especially since I won't see him for two days.

"Babe." He puts his arms around me and rests his head on my shoulder. "I'm sorry. I'm just in my head too much and I'm going to miss you. I don't want anything to come between us, and I feel like the odds are against us right now." There is a sadness in his voice.

"Just trust me." I turn around and put my arms around his neck. "Trust us." I kiss his lips softly.

"I'll try." He kisses me again.

We stand silently for a few moments, taking in the scenery of the lake and a couple boats that pass through in the distance.

"Now let's quit all this and enjoy our time together." He starts laughing and scoops me up in his arms and starts walking towards the water.

"Put me down! Put me down right now, Clay Keller," I yell as I kick my legs and try and free myself. I know exactly what he's thinking. He's laughing but I am shrieking at the thought of him throwing me in.

He sets me down and I feel a rush of relief.

"You jerk." I swat him playfully. "I thought for sure—"

He grabs me again and he does it—he jumps into the lake with me in his arms and both of us fully clothed.

"Clay! I can't believe you just did that!" I howl as he laughs and starts splashing me. I put my hands on his head, trying to push him down, but he grabs my arms and kisses me.

"You're cute when you're mad." He wipes water away from my eyes. I wrap my legs around him and realize what's done is done, so I might as well make the best of it. "I love you," he says as he moves his lips over my neck.

"Please don't ever stop." I run my fingers through his wet brown hair.

"Stop what?"

"Loving me," I answer and press my lips into his.

He breathes into my ear. "Never."

The clouds are moving overhead and the sky is getting dark when raindrops begin falling on us. "We better get out of here," I tell him.

"Why? We're already wet." He laughs at me.

While that is true enough, I've always been scared of swimming—even taking showers—during storms. A loud boom makes me jump. "*That's* why!"

We swim to shore as the rain really begins to come down. Clay takes my hand and we hurry to his truck. He slams the tailgate shut, and we jump in while laughing at ourselves. We have no towels or extra clothes so I cover up with a blanket from the backseat and Clay turns the heat on. He pulls me over to him and onto his lap and the water from my drenched clothes seeps into him.

"Look what you've done to us." I pull at my wet shirt.

He smirks. "You liked it."

In the heat of the moment, I pull my uncomfortable shirt over my head and throw it on the passenger floorboard.

"Mmmm," Clay hums and brings his lips to my chest, right above my bra. "Why are you teasing me?"

"It's your fault. You got my shirt all wet." I joke as I lean my head back, and he kisses his way up to my neck—

—when a sudden thud on the driver's side window startles us both.

"Dad," I choke.

Chapter Fifteen

I push myself off Clay's lap and climb over to the passenger's side, retrieving my shirt from the floor and trying to get it back on my sticky and still wet body. "Oh my God, Clay! What do we do? What do I say?"

"Out of the truck, Iris." I hear Dad's stern voice.

I'm panicking now. I open the door and slide out with my head down. I feel humiliated.

"Dad. What are you doing here?" I ask, still looking at the ground, knowing that he'd just seen me on top of Clay topless.

"I tried calling you and you didn't answer. I got worried. What the hell is going on here?" He demands answers. His arms are crossed in front of him and I know he is furious.

My phone! I reach in my back pocket and pull out my soaked phone. *Oh, no!*

"Well, that explains it. I guess that's what irresponsibility gets you. It's also going to cost you your job if you keep this up."

What does this have to do with my job? Wait—I was supposed to work the evening shift today. I completely forgot that I picked up the extra hours. I've been so busy getting ready for our trip tomorrow and my mind has been in a fog.

I put my hands over my face. "I'll call Mrs. Jones," I tell him.

Clay is sitting silently in the truck and I don't blame him. This situation is more than awkward for all of us.

"Get your car and we will talk at home." He begins walking to his truck.

I walk over to the driver's side and Clay rolls down his window. I wait until Dad pulls away to speak. Then I lay my head down on the windowsill and let out a sigh.

"That was... um. Unexpected." I pull out my phone and hold it up to show him.

"Oh, shit," he curses. "I didn't know you had your phone in your pocket."

"I didn't even think about it. I also completely forgot that I had to work."

"They'll get over it." He tries to make me feel better, but it doesn't help.

"Clay, it's important to me. I have never even been late for a shift, let alone missed one." I suddenly feel like I am losing control of everything that means anything to me. I am disappointing my dad; I paid for this phone that is now ruined; and now I've shirked my work.

He brushes the hair away from my forehead. "It will all blow over. I'll get you a new phone, it's my fault."

"No, no. I'll get a new one eventually," I tell him. "But now? I better get going." And I start to walk away.

"Hey," he yells as I turn around, feeling defeated. "I love you."

"I love you, too." I give him half a smile.

Dad is sitting at the kitchen table by the time I get home, and I go into my room to change before he lashes out at me. Once I'm all dry, I figure I might as well get this over with. Lily and Rose are home, too, so I know they will be eavesdropping from the living room.

"Dad." I take a seat across from him. "I'm so sorry."

"Iris, you're an adult now so your private life isn't my business. But you have to remember that every choice has a consequence." He speaks softly and it only adds to the feeling of his disappointment in me.

"I honestly just got my days mixed up. I'm not used to the evening shift and..." He puts his hand up to stop me.

"This isn't about work. I know you are a hard worker and I don't doubt that. This is about that boy," he says.

Calling him *that boy* sounds strange, considering Dad has known Clay since he was born. I guess now that he has to keep a closer eye on him, he is considered "that boy."

"He's not a just a boy, Dad. He's changed a lot and he's been really good to me." I try and talk Clay up, completely aware of the fact that Dad knows how all of the Keller boys have been to me in the past. He's had to pull me off the ground crying after some of their antics.

"Just be careful, Iris. I was your age when I met your mom and I know how a young man's mind works."

If he only knew. Clay and I have already been together a handful of times.

"I am, Dad. Trust me, OK?" I smile.

Dad gets up and walks over to me and gives me a hug. I wasn't expecting him to be so understanding, but he is right—I'm an adult now, and I need to start acting like it.

Lily and Rose make their way into the kitchen and Dad leaves. They both sit at the table and stare at me. "We need details."

I fill them in on every embarrassing detail of our dad finding me shirtless on top of Clay, and they think it's hilarious, while I blush even retelling it.

"Our baby sister is growing up," Lily laughs and puts her arms around my head.

"Quit it, you two!"

I really should call Mrs. Jones to explain that I got my days mixed up, which is true. I apologize, and she tells me not to worry about it and that she got me covered.

I wake up the next morning to the sound of Dad shouting. He rarely shouts, so I rush downstairs to see what's going on, and find him having a very heated conversation on the phone. He should be at work and the fact that he's not makes me very nervous. I sit at the kitchen table, and for a time, he doesn't realize I am there.

I can't understand what any of the conversation is about, but soon, he slams the phone down and rests his head on his hands upon the countertop.

"Dad, is everything OK?" I put my hand on his shoulder.

He jumps up, startled by my presence. "Iris, how long were you standing there?"

"Not long," I tell him. "What was the all about? Why aren't you at work?"

"It was nothing. I had to take care of some stuff this morning at the bank. I'm heading to work now."

He assures me that everything is OK, but I have serious, blood-curdling doubts. I don't bother to ask, though, because he wouldn't tell me. Dad doesn't like to burden me with any problems he thinks are out of my control. He kisses my forehead and takes the lunch I made for him and leaves for work.

I wish there was a way I could find out what is going on. Maybe I should talk to Mr. Radley. If Dad loses his job, then we will lose everything. He's already had to give up possession of the farm he loves; he would be devastated if he wasn't able to work there.

There is no way I will be able to go to college if he loses his job. I'll have to find something that pays better and help out with bills. The overwhelming weight on my shoulders feels like it is pushing me into the ground.

After lunch, I decide to walk over to the farm, just to make sure he is, in fact, working. I see Dad's truck parked at the main barn and notice him outside with a familiar man. I walk up a little closer through the pasture; the tall dead grass feels itchy on my bare legs. It's Mr. Keller. *Why would Dad be talking to Mr. Keller at work,* I wonder, hoping this has nothing to do with Clay.

I try to get a little closer so I can hear what they're talking about. Dad doesn't seem angry anymore, but sad and desperate. I can't make out what they are saying except for something about a loan. Some kind of loan for the house? I still can't figure out what Mr. Keller has to do with any of this, and can only dread it has to do with me.

I slouch down into the tall grass and sneak back through the dividing pasture to my house. When I get there, I spot Clay's truck parked at the end of the driveway. He has some balls to show up here after yesterday but he probably knew my dad wasn't around. I wonder if he might know what's going on with our parents.

"Hi, babe." He kisses my cheek when I reach the front porch.

"Hey, what's going on?" I ask, expecting something to be wrong.

"I brought you something." He brings his hands around and he's holding a small gift bag.

"You got me a present?" I exclaim. "But why?"

"Just open it." I take the bag from him and pull out a piece of yellow tissue paper and inside is a box. I pull it out, and it's a brand-new cell phone—one of the latest models. "I owed you a one," he says.

My mouth drops open. "Clay, this is too much. You shouldn't have done this," I murmur as I put the box back into the bag and try handing it back to him.

He doesn't take it. "Yes, I should have. I ruined your other one. Besides, I need to be able to tell you goodnight when you are gone." He places his hands on my arms and pushes them towards me while I hold the bag.

"I have something for you, too." I smile, wanting to give him a present in return. "Stay right here."

I walk briskly into the house and grab my book off my bed, returning to Clay with it held behind my back. And then hand it to him. I had planned to just give him the book, anyway, since I know our days together will exceed the numbers of chapters. I even wrote something special for him in the end, and I hope that we can continue to write *our* book together.

"Read this whenever you start to miss me." I smile. "I know the deal was a chapter for each day together, but I plan to see you more than the twenty-three chapters in this book."

"I like the way you think." He kisses my cheek.

I throw myself into his arms and thank him at least ten times. We go inside, and he helps me get it all set up with my old phone plan.

"You know, I've never seen your bedroom." He winks at me.

"No!" I insist. "The last thing we need is to get caught in another uncomfortable position."

"What kind of position would that be?" He grabs me by the waist and pulls me into him, kissing my ear. "Your dad is at work."

"But my sisters are here," I laugh. "Besides, your dad is over at the farm talking to my dad as we speak. Any idea why?"

He gives me an odd look. "Not that I can think of. Unless your dad is trying to tell my dad to keep me away from you."

"I don't think my dad would do that." I grimace. "Maybe your dad wants you to stay away from me."

"My dad is pretty pissed at me right now, but it has nothing to do with you." He sits down in a chair and pulls me into his lap.

"Why? What happened?"

"It's nothing. I missed a couple days of my internship and my dad found out."

I pull away. "Clay, why? You worked so hard for that internship," I remember, feeling slightly disappointed in him.

"I was busy. With you."

I gasp and put my hand to my head. "Maybe we need to slow down a little bit. I don't want to, but we are both making some poor choices lately. We should be building each other up, and instead, we're dragging each other down."

"What? No!" He turns my face to his. "We are just fine."

When he kisses my lips, I regret even saying that. I can't go slower. I already feel like I can't get enough of him.

"We just really need to stay focused. Both of us." I kiss him again. "I don't want to be the reason you lose your internship."

"I'm not going to lose anything and we certainly aren't going to slow down. If anything, we need to speed up." He tickles my sides and I squirm on his lap. But then Rose walks in, and we both stop.

"Aren't you two just the cutest." She giggles.

"I'll walk you out," I tell Clay as I stand up to take his hand.

At the door, away from my sister's eyes, I wrap my arms around his neck and kiss him over and over again. "I'll miss you."

"I'll miss you more," he says in between kisses. Then he laughs impishly and gives me a slap on the butt before walking away.

I sit on the porch step and wave to him as he pulls away, and when I can no longer see him, I lie back and smile. I feel like the luckiest girl in the world in this moment. I have everything I have ever wanted and more.

Chapter Sixteen

The drive to Seattle goes quickly. I distract myself by playing around on my new phone and updating my Facebook status to *in a relationship,* and hope Clay doesn't mind. I get a lot of congrats, and a few of my friends are very surprised. I'm surprised, too. “Rainbow” by Kacey Musgraves is playing on the radio, and I sink back into the seat, because the song really makes me think.

I'm reminded of the rain in the lake with Clay, and I feel my face turn red when I think about how that turned out. My mind then wanders to the other struggles of life—just trying to stay above water and get by. All I have ever done is try to get by.

Up until now, I’ve never done much of anything for myself without thinking of everyone else. I need to take down the umbrella and enjoy the rainbow over my head. There is so much beauty in this world and I want to see it, I want to feel it. The warmth of the sun on my skin at a beach, the adrenaline rush of climbing a mountain, the excitement of getting a good grade in a college exam. I need to do these things. I smile to myself at the thoughts of my future with Clay, but they’re chased with a hint of sadness when I think about being away from him when he goes back to school. I know that I cannot push my dreams away so that I can make him happy—just like I shouldn't have to for Dad. If they love me, and I know they do, then they will encourage me to do this for myself.

My phone beeps its annoying beep. It's a text from Clay.

What's up with your new Facebook status?

A rush of worry comes over me. Maybe I shouldn't have done that.

I type quickly: *I figured I would change it since I'm no longer single anymore???? Neither are you!*

I'm not trying to be possessive, but there is no reason for either of us to pretend to be single online. Outside the world of my phone, we're already pulling into the driveway of Aunt Meg's—I tell the girls I'll meet them inside.

Another message from Clay is waiting:

Our relationship isn't anyone's business though.

I don't understand what the big deal is, I reply.

It's not a big deal but now my phone is blowing up with messages from people asking a bunch of questions.

And? If it's no one's business then ignore them. Oh, I add. Let me guess...Lexi?

Damn that girl. She better not try to interfere.

Amongst others.

I ask again. *So, Lexi is messaging you?*

No response but: *I gotta go.*

What the hell? I open my Facebook page, and Clay has denied the request to add me as his *partner* in a relationship.

You deleted it? Fine! I text. *I guess you can have fun being single!*

I should feel hurt, but I'm too angry and confused. I can't help but feel like Clay is doing this because of Lexi. I don't know why he even talks to her after what she did. I feel jealous and want to know what he said to her.

Quit being childish, he writes to me.

Yeah, because I'm the one being childish. Goodbye, Clay.

I grab my bag and go in the house, where I throw it down, feeling the eyes of Becca and my sisters keenly upon me. "Where's the party at tonight?"

"Where is Iris and who is this girl?" Becca runs to me and wraps her arms around me.

Fury is building inside me and I have a desire both to grab Clay's attention and get to him the way he's getting to me.

"I know just the place," Becca says as she carries my bag to the spare bedroom.

We all get ready and I wear a cute black dress of Becca's. It's much too revealing, but being in the city makes me feel like I can let loose a little bit. I wear a pair of her black platform sandals and put the makeup on a little heavier this time. My hair flows straight down the open back of the dress.

We all look like we are heading to a nightclub, but Becca decides to take us to a summer frat party off campus by UW. I have never been to a frat party, so I'm pretty nervous.

When we arrive, I decide to have one glass of the fruity red punch that is in a trash can, just to lighten up a little. I triple-check that it isn't a *used* trash can at least three times before I drink it. The alcohol is strong, and I have no idea what it is but it goes down smoothly.

I'm finishing my cup when a tall and very attractive blond approaches. His baby-blue eyes match his button-up. He takes my cup from me, refills it, and hands it back. "I've never seen you around before."

"I've never been here. I'm with Becca." I point to her where she's hanging on the arm of another gorgeous guy. They are everywhere!

"Ahh, Becca." He laughs.

"You know her?" I ask as I take another sip.

"Oh, yeah, we all know Becca." He turns around and looks at her again. I'm not really sure what he meant by that, and it must show on my face. "What I mean is she comes here a lot. She's with him." He points. "Rex."

I hold out my hand. "I'm Iris."

"Jackson." He accepts my hand and kisses the top of it, making me blush a little, before walking away.

I'm having a really good time, but I'm starting to miss Clay. I find myself over on a couch sulking and checking to see if he's sent me a text. Nothing. I start to think about what he might be doing, and then I begin to think the worst—that maybe he's with Lexi—and the fury comes back. I get up off the couch and walk over to get another drink where Jackson is standing. Feeling like I need to shake Clay, I spark up another conversation with this handsome stranger, and then pull out my phone to take a picture of us as he kisses my cheek while my mouth draws into the shape of an 'O.' I'm starting to feel a little more fearless—or irresponsible, as Dad would say, and I post the picture on my Facebook page, hoping that Clay sees it. He is right—I *am* being childish right now—but I don't know how to handle these feelings I have.

I go to find my cousin and sisters, and we all dance with a large group. While I'm walking to the kitchen for another drink, my phone beeps in the tiny wristlet I borrowed from Becca. It's Clay.

Where the hell are you? he texts.

I guess I got his attention. *Oh,* I sass, *now you want to talk?*

I wander outside into the grass and there are just as many people outside as there are inside. I look up and type the words I see on the front of the house: *Alpha Delta Phi.*

Whatever that means. I don't know much about fraternities, but I assume Alpha means leader.

Who was the guy in the picture?

My new friend, I fob.

What the hell, Iris!

What? You're single, right? That means I'm mingle

Oops, I laugh at myself and try to correct the mistake:

tingle

Once more:

SINGLE haha

Clay doesn't seem as amused as I am. All he writes in reply is: *Are you drunk?*

I think I might be, I concur.

Damnit Iris! I'm coming to get you.

Nope, you're not because you're too busy with Lexi.

I hope he doesn't really come here. As much as I want to see him right now and as happy as I am that my plan worked, I don't want him to cause a scene. He won't come, anyways. He probably really is busy with Lexi.

Clay doesn't respond, so I decide to go back in the house, and suddenly I start to feel very ill. I've only had three drinks, but I'm not sure how much liquor was in them, and I can't handle much. I push my way through the crowd and finally find a bathroom just in time before it all comes out.

I sit back on the floor and lean my head against a wall, thinking about how many people have probably thrown up in this disgusting bathroom. I force myself up and wash my hands.

It's later when I manage to find Lily, our designated driver, and convince her to take me back to Aunt Meg's. I'm still feeling pretty sick in the car, too, so she has to pull over while I throw up again. I wipe my mouth with a napkin on the floor and hold it in my hand in case I need it again.

A message blinks on my phone.

I can't find the frat house. Which road is it on?

Shit, he actually drove here! He must have sped to make it that fast.

I'm going back to my aunt's, I explain. *Not feeling very good.*

Send me the address.

When we pull into the driveway, Clay is already there. As soon as I open the door, the gas station water Lily stopped to get me wears off, and I begin throwing up again. Clay rushes over to me and holds my hair.

"How much did she drink?" he asks.

"Honestly, I don't think she drank that much. Hopefully she's not pregnant," she jokes.

I look up at her and roll my eyes. "It's the alcohol."

Lily leaves and Clay helps me inside.

I go in the spare bedroom to change and brush my teeth while Clay waits in the living room. Suddenly feeling very hungry since I emptied my stomach numerous times, I grab a granola bar from the cupboard and a big glass of water.

"Why did you come here?" I sit down cross-legged on the couch next to Clay.

"Because! You posted a picture of another guy kissing you." He shakes his head. "You told me I didn't have to worry about this."

"It was nothing. I don't even know the guy and he only kissed my cheek." I take a bite of my granola bar. "Besides, you didn't seem like you cared what I did earlier."

"I just didn't think it was necessary for everyone to know what was going on with us."

"Or could it be that you're embarrassed to be dating the likes of me." I bring my hands up to my chest.

"No, Iris. I love you and I'm proud to be with you. I just don't want people trying to put their nose in our business and causing problems."

I laugh bitterly. "Yeah, OK. We are either together or we're not. If we are, then there is no reason to hide it. I'm not playing these games."

He sits back into the couch and rubs his face in exasperation. "Of course we are together. If it makes you happy, I'll change my status."

My smile is enormous. "Yep, that would make me happy."

"But you can't run off and get drunk and let other guys kiss you every time we have a disagreement, because then we will not be together. I mean it, Iris." He sounds serious, and I nod. He is right. I knew exactly what I was doing, and it was wrong, but here he is. Here we are.

"Where were you at tonight?" I ask him.

"I was at home. I played basketball at the gym for a while and then went home for the rest of the night," he explains, and I feel awful assuming he was with Lexi. The alcohol made me think all sorts of craziness, and now that I've sobered up, I see how foolish I was.

"I'm sorry." I put my arms around him and lay my head on his chest. "I'm glad you're here, though."

"I'm sorry, too." He kisses my head.

"Will you stay with me?" I ask him. I know my aunt would kill me if she knew, but she won't be back until tomorrow night, and the girls won't care.

"I guess I can stay. I did drive two hours to save you; I might as well," he laughs.

"Save me, huh?" I look up at him.

"Yes, from drunken fraternity guys who might take advantage of a hot little thing like you." He pulls me into his lap and starts kissing my neck. It turns me on, but I feel it would be wildly disrespectful to do anything at my aunt's house, so I pull him away and tell him not tonight. He begs a little but finally gives up trying.

The next morning, I have to keep nudging Clay to shut his phone up. After the third round of beeps, he finally silences it, and we fall back asleep. An hour later, I wake up to Clay looking over at me.

I cover my face. "What are you doing?"

"Just watching you sleep."

I chuckle. "And listening to me snore?"

"Nope, not this time. You do move your lips a little bit when you sleep and you smiled a couple of times." He smiles at me and kisses me. "I'm probably going to get going soon. I'm already late for work."

"You have to work today? It's already nine o'clock! You're supposed to be there at seven!" I jump up.

"Yeah, I'll be a little late but they'll get over it. It's Saturday, so there's only one guy in today and he's pretty chill."

I completely forgot that Clay has to work the first Saturday of every month, and I feel guilty for causing him to come all this way. "I'm so sorry for last night. Do you forgive me?" I frown out a pout.

"Of course I do." He flops onto his back on the bed.

"Good, because there's something I need to talk to you about later. Can I come over when I get back to town?"

"What is it? You can't say that and then leave me wondering all day. Did you do something with that guy?" He sits up stiffly, immediately upset.

"No! It's nothing like that. It has to do with my future and school." He really does have trust issues and insecurities because of Lexi. Damn that girl, I could slap her for hurting him so bad.

"Oh, good." He stands up and pulls me into him. "As anxious as I am to hear all about it, I really do have to go, so I'll text you when I'm home from work." He kisses my forehead goodbye.

Clay leaves and the girls join me in the kitchen while I make pancakes. Everyone except Lily is feeling a little under the weather today. Becca decides she's going back to bed, so we pack up and head back home.

Lily and Rose take a little detour to show me the resident halls at Bellevue, and I can see myself feeling at home there. It's like a little community of separate tiny apartments, but we aren't able to go inside because the girls didn't pay for summer housing. Bellevue College doesn't look too big and intimidating, unlike Washington State. I feel like I would be a small fish in a big ocean at State.

The drive back feels long this time. I log into Facebook and delete the picture I posted last night, feeling remorseful. I still can't believe I did that to Clay.

There's a notification waiting, and when I click it, the message makes me grin from ear to ear. Clay changed his relationship status. My heart melts into a puddle of mush and I begin to miss him even more than I already did.

I feel like I am floating on air, my heart and soul are so full of love for this man. It almost seems too good to be true, but we've worked hard to get to where we are. It was destined to be from the very beginning, I think. The thought of losing him is gut-wrenching and I fear that someday I may. After losing my mom, I have a fear of loss instilled in me that has protected my heart ever since, and now that I am taking a leap of faith, I pray that I am not blindsided.

Chapter Seventeen

CLAY

When I finally get to work after the long-ass drive from Seattle, my supervisor is already in a bad mood.

"Start gathering the supplies on this list for Monday's project." He slams it into my chest. This is my first Saturday working with this guy and I can already that he's going to be a pain in the ass. If only he was as chill as I told Iris he'd be.

Thinking of Iris gets me distracted and I start stacking the wrong size boards. "Damnit!" I shout, starting all over.

The way her beautiful blonde hair falls perfectly around her face and the way she smiles right away when we wake up together—she's perfection. I've known it all along, I just wish I wouldn't have taken so long to pursue her. There are so many years in-between that we could have spent together. I get agitated at the thought of anyone or anything coming between us. Iris thinks that I didn't accept that stupid *relationship request* shit because I was ashamed, but that is far from the truth. The truth is I fear that the more people know, the more they will try and ruin us, Lexi being the main culprit. I know too well how vengeful she can be, and the thought of her hurting Iris infuriates me. Now that I've deleted her and blocked her from all of my accounts, maybe she will leave me alone. I thought we could try and be civil towards each other, given that we hang out in the same group, but she has proven that's not possible.

"You better pick up the pace if you want to make up for your lost hours today," James says. I don't know how I'm going to handle working with this prick all summer. During the week, there are a couple other interns here for him to ride, but Saturdays it's just one-a-month.

"Got it, boss." I give him a salute and flip him off when he turns around. I usually don't let people get under my skin, but this guy does it. I suppose I haven't been the most reliable employee, which is out-of-character for me. I've always been an overachiever, but this lovestruck shit has me all messed up.

I got a call from my boss a few days ago, and he warned me that if I miss one more day, then I'm terminated from my internship—and I went ahead and screwed up again today. At least I made it in, though, so I'm hopeful he'll cut me some slack. If I lose this job, I can kiss my dad's tuition payment help goodbye. On top of that, Iris would likely blame herself and worry she's dragging me down when, in reality, she's the only thing keeping me together.

"Pick up the pace, Keller," James shouts from his office. He can't even see me. I could be completely done and he wouldn't even know it. Damn, doesn't this guy have work to do? I've made it my new goal to work my ass off so I can take his boss's job when he retires, just so I can chop *his* balls every day.

The next two hours go slow as hell, but I survived my first Saturday with Sergeant Shithead, and I'm thankful I don't have to do it again for another month.

As soon as I get in my truck, I turn my phone on to see how Iris is doing.

Hey babe, how was the ride home?

Long, she answers, *but I fell asleep halfway and then it went quick.*

I'm leaving work now if you wanna come over and talk about whatever you needed to.

Give me an hour, I just have to finish laundry.

Sounds good. I love you.

I love you, too... and I miss you already.

Same babe, can't wait to see you.

She leaves me with *xoxo*.

I still remember the first time I kissed her. I was left out of my brothers' roughhousing with his friends as usual, so I wanted to try and get their attention, and the only way I ever could was by doing something funny. I acted like I was going to give Iris a kiss and stuck a toad on her. My brother and his buddies laughed their asses off, but when Iris ran off crying, I had to go after her.

It was my first kiss and I knew it was hers, but when our lips touched, it felt like the most natural thing ever, like we'd done it one hundred times before. I turned around and walked away so she didn't see the bulge in my pants but I had a big smile on my face and I knew she was the one for me.

The day we moved, I remember looking up at her in her window while she watched and I could see the sadness in her eyes. I knew she liked me, too, and that made me smile and in return it made her smile. I made a promise to myself that I would do anything to bring that smile out in her, but I failed miserably. We grew older and we grew apart, but I had always hoped one day we would grow back together, and we have.

When I pull into my driveway, I slap my hands onto my steering wheel. Luke is home. That fucker better not say a word to me. I'm tired of him thinking that we can pretend nothing happened. I've told him—just like I told my parents—I'll tolerate his presence because we are all family, but I will not be his friend. My parents understand the reasoning behind my feelings towards Luke, but naturally, they want to see us reconcile. It's just not in the cards right now.

The house smells like cinnamon rolls, so I assume Mom is baking. I say hello and kiss her cheek. "Iris is coming over soon. Will you let me know when she gets here?"

"Sure, honey. Hey, what's going on with you two?" she asks as she wipes her hands on her apron.

"I love her," I spit but don't regret it.

She smiles. "Love, huh?"

"Yep, I really do." I smile back.

"Well, maybe since you have moved on with Iris, then you can let go of what happened with Lexi and Luke." She tilts her head.

"I don't wanna talk about this right now. Just send Iris in my room when she gets here, *please*." I walk in my room and shut the door. I know Mom means well, but I need a lot more time and space than they are giving me. I've moved on from what Lexi did; she can fuck fifty guys for all I care. It's Luke's actions I can't get passed.

I decide to take a quick shower before Iris gets here, and when I walk back into my room, she's lying on my bed with her knees bent up and her nose in a book she's reading. "Hey." She smiles.

"Sorry you had to wait. I thought I had time to take a quick shower." I run the towel over my damp hair and throw it on the floor.

"It's no problem. I talked with your mom for a few minutes and she played Twenty Questions with me." She laughs and closes her book.

"Oh, boy. I don't even want to know." I start laughing. I imagine Mom wanted all the details. She has always adored Iris, so I'm sure she's beside herself. Dad—not so much. When I came home for the summer, he warned me to stay away from girls and pull my shit back together before I go back to school.

Iris looks absolutely beautiful today. I'm unsure how I denied that beauty for so long. She's far better-looking than any of the girls I've dated in the past, and don't get me started on that body. I can't seem to keep my hands off her when she's around. I throw myself into her on the bed and the sound of her laugh echoing in my ears pleases me. Her unique ability to make everyone around her smile is intriguing all on its own, but mixed with her stubbornness and sometimes clumsy antics, she is the prime example of a perfect imperfection. I'll make it my lifelong goal to keep this girl happy.

"OK." She puts her face in her hands as she sits up, and I can tell she's nervous. "I need to talk to you about school."

I pull her hands away and hold them in mine. "You made a decision?"

"It's never really been a decision to make. Honestly, Clay, I don't want to go to State. I'm not saying that I'm going to Bellevue yet, but I can tell you with certainty that I'm not going to State."

She looks sad now and I feel like I need to fix it, but I'm not sure how. I need her with me and I fear this won't work if she's not.

"I know you don't." It's all I can say. I can't force her to go and I can see that she really doesn't want to.

"Are you upset?" She frowns and I put my hand on her cheek.

"No, we will make it work." I smile.

Chapter Eighteen

IRIS

I know he's disappointed, but he is remaining calm and hasn't told me we are over yet, so I'm feeling optimistic. The more and more I think about it, I'm leaning towards going to Bellevue, but I need to talk to Dad before I make any decisions.

"So, Bellevue, huh?" Clay looks down and starts tracing the lines in his comforter.

"I'm not really sure yet but I'm thinking so," I tell him as I sit crossed-legged on his bed and twirl my hair around my finger.

"What if I came with you," he asks.

"What? No! Clay, you go to a great school and your parents would never allow it." I can't believe he's even thinking like this.

"My parents don't get to decide where I go to school. Besides, there are too many distractions at State. I can get a degree at Bellevue." He lays his head back into his pillow.

"Clay, you're talking crazy right now. We've only been together for a month." I begin laughing because saying it out loud makes it sound even more ridiculous.

"Why are you laughing? I'm dead serious. I know this will work." He's staring at me now like he's waiting for a reaction.

"I...I don't know what to say. I guess you can do whatever you want, but I think we will be just fine. You finish out at State while I'm at Bellevue and we can see each other during breaks. It's not like I'll be on the other side of the country. We will be fine," I assure him.

He stares back at the ceiling. "Maybe you're right. It was a silly idea."

I feel pretty bad for laughing at him because he seemed sincere, but I don't want him making such a drastic change for our relationship. If we are meant to be, like I think we are, then we can survive a couple years of being away from each other.

"I love you." I lay my head next to his and run my fingers through his hair.

He stays silent and I feel like he may be upset with me. "Are you mad?" I ask.

"I'm not mad, I just expected a different reaction."

"I said I love you." I begin kissing his cheek over and over trying to cheer him up.

"I love you, too." He turns his head and puts his lips to mine.

We spend the remainder of the night lying in bed watching a movie. I decide to tell Dad that I'm staying at Amber's again and that I'll be missing church. This is the second Sunday I've missed, and I'm feeling pretty guilty about my lies. Clay insists that his parents won't care if I stay, but I'm not leaving this room all night at the risk of seeing them.

The next morning, I decide to shower here since his parents are at church. Clay makes me breakfast again, but today, it's toaster waffles.

"One day I'm going to cook you breakfast." I smile as I stick my fork into a waffle and put a bite in my mouth.

Clay's phone starts vibrating on the table and he reaches over and grabs it.

"Shit, I forgot I told Bryce I'd play ball with them today. Do you wanna come watch?"

"Eh, I'm not sure. Bryce doesn't like me very much." I like that Clay is willing to bring me around his friends now, but I don't feel like being belittled by them.

He rubs my arm in a comforting way. "Don't worry about him. If he says anything remotely rude to you, I'll put him in his place."

"OK." I smile. I like the idea of watching Clay in his element, playing basketball. He's always been very athletic and sports were his passion in school, so I want to be a part of that.

Clay goes to change and walks out to the kitchen in gray gym shorts and his Washington State T-shirt. He looks so attractive in gym clothes. He looks attractive in anything.

We swing by my house so I can run in and change my clothes. I linger over my choices in my closet and pull out a yellow sun dress at first, but tuck it back away when the memory of Bryce's humiliating words bites me. I open up my dresser drawer and feel confident with a pair dark blue twill shorts and a white V-neck.

There are a lot more people than I imagined at the gym, and I feel like a bit of a loner. Three girls sit in the bleachers talking amongst themselves; I recognize them all from the class ahead of me. Six guys are on the floor playing basketball, Bryce among them. Clay kisses me on the cheek and goes out to the floor, and I sit by myself on the second row near the door, playing around on my phone so I'm not just sitting here alone doing nothing. I text Lily to make sure my sisters are OK with making dinner, and they assure me everything is fine. I feel like I've been neglecting my household chores lately and I need to start spending a little more time at home.

I discover Eric sent me a Facebook invitation to his graduation party next weekend. It's the same weekend as Amber's open house, so I note it in my calendar and determine to make a day of it. Those are probably the only two events I'll attend.

I take a couple pictures of Clay playing basketball and then look back at them on my phone and smile.

"He looks good when he plays, doesn't he?" Lexi sits down next to me.

I look up and notice Clay glancing over at us. He looks pissed.

I smile and hope she will just go away. "Yeah, sure."

"You know, when we were together, I watched every practice and he never even thanked me for it. It's like he expected me to," she says.

Why is she telling me this?

"He's always been very self-absorbed."

"He's always treated me with nothing but respect." I smile devilishly. If he was self-absorbed, he wouldn't have offered to go to Bellevue just to be near me.

"It won't last," she chuckles. "Give it a couple months and he will get bored and start ditching you to hang out with someone new, just like he did to me."

"You're the one who did that to him," I snap. "Not vice versa."

"Is that what he told you?" She laughs. "Figures he would put all the blame on me. That's how he is. Clay Keller does nothing wrong."

"Enlighten me," I say, curious about what actually happened, even if I won't believe it.

"Clay and I left for school together last fall and everything was great until, one night after drinking, I woke up in his bed and he was gone. I walked back to my dorm to get my phone so I could call him and found him in bed... with my dorm mate. He swears nothing happened, but I didn't buy it."

Clay never told me any of this. I don't expect him to give me every detail of their relationship, but surely I'd expect him to tell me if he was unfaithful.

"What about you and Luke?"

"Well, Clay and I stayed together, but I never fully got over it. I finished my semester early and came home before him, got drunk, ended up sleeping with Luke at a party and my so-called friends ratted me out. That was the end. Sort of." She smiles.

She speaks of it all so casually, like it was no big deal.

"Sort of?" I ask as I continue to watch Clay. We make eye contact a couple times.

"We still hooked up a few times. Just a few weeks ago, actually." She looks at me with a smile and knows she just got me.

My insides are burning now and I need answers. "A few weeks ago? When?"

"Right before Mark's party. You know, the one where you got drunk and swindled him away from me for the night."

"I didn't *swindle* him away from you. He tracked me down at a bonfire and came back to my house. He did that all on his own." I feel my anger rising. How could Clay do that? I know we weren't together, but it was at the beginning, where I was thinking of him day and night and he was slowly making me fall for him. It was the very same night we stayed up talking for hours and I shared some of my most intimate thoughts with him. I feel sick, and I have to get out of here.

I stand up and rush out of the gym and head straight for the exit. I keep looking back to make sure Clay isn't following me, and when I am outside, I turn a corner and call Rose to come pick me up. It's too far to walk home.

I can't compete with Lexi. She's everything that I'm not. She's confident and pretty and she has a way of getting everyone to do exactly what she wants. She's probably convincing Clay to take her home right now.

Just as Rose pulls up, Clay comes busting out the door and rushes over to me and I walk as fast I can to Rose's car and get in the passenger side, shutting the door.

"Go," I say.

Chapter Nineteen

CLAY

"What the hell did you say to her," I shout at Lexi as she sits twiddling her thumbs with a pleased look on her face. I shout louder: "What did you say?"

She looks up at me with her cold dark eyes. "I just told her the truth."

I have to find her. I throw the ball down and run out of the gym and stop to look around—she's not here. I walk out the door and I see her getting into her sister's car.

"Fuck!" I yell and put my hands on the top of my head. I go back into the gym to grab my phone and my keys.

On my way, I point at Lexi. "Stay away from us."

"Us?" She laughs. "It's cute and all but you two will never work. You'll screw up and she will leave you. She's too good for you, Clay." She smiles like she feels accomplished in trying to sabotage my relationship.

I tell the guys I gotta go and get in my truck and try and call Iris a couple times, but as I expected, she doesn't answer, so I text her.

Don't listen to anything Lexi says. She's just trying to destroy us. Please don't let her.

I sit for a minute and wait for a response.

Did you sleep with her the day of graduation?

I knew that's what she told her. Iris and I weren't even together then. It shouldn't matter but I know it does.

Yeah, but that was before.

Before what? Before you started showing up at my house randomly? Before you pulled me away from a party because you thought something might happen between me and another guy? Before you kissed me?

I'm sorry. If I knew what I know now it never would have happened. I can't take it back. I wish I could.

Did you cheat on Lexi with her roommate? she demands.

What? No! Lexi doesn't believe me but I swear nothing happened that night. I was drunk and couldn't handle Lexi's bitchiness so I went back to her room to sleep. Somehow I ended up on the wrong bed and her roommate must have got in bed with me in it. I woke up to Lexi slapping me across the face.

That sounds like a big misunderstanding and she should have trusted you, Iris writes, and relief flushes through me. She goes on: *But I just need some time right now. I'll call you later and we can talk about this.*

OK, I agree. I can give you some time but please don't take too long, I miss you already.

She doesn't respond so I decide to give her space. I need to put an end to this thing with Lexi once and for all.

I go back in the gym and everyone is still there, including Lexi. I take her by the arm and she follows me into the hall.

"This ends now." I look straight into her eyes with the same tone I used when I told her we were done in the first place. "I'm with Iris now and nothing you do can change that."

"It won't last." She crosses her arms.

"I intend to do everything I can to ensure that it does. I love her." There, I said it—maybe now she will see that I'm serious about this.

"Love?" She laughs. "You told me the same thing."

"You're right, I did and I shouldn't have. Now that I know what love actually feels like, I realize that I was never in love with you." I can see the sadness in her eyes, but it's the truth. I know that Lexi had real feelings for me, as I thought I did for her, but the minute she slept with my brother, I realized it wasn't real. Iris has opened my eyes to a whole new world of possibilities and has shown me what true love is.

"What do you see in her? She's so... *plain* and boring." She rolls her eyes and looks down at her nails.

"You may look at her like that but I see so much more. You don't know a thing about her. She's real and that's something you will never be." I know I keep digging the knife deeper but

I need her to get the bigger picture here. She's my past; Iris is my future. Lexi has never caught a glimpse of her smiling in her sleep or watched her excitement at saving a nest of baby birds. She's never seen the way Iris is always willing to lend a helping hand, whether it's a complete stranger or a member of her family. She doesn't know Iris is the definition of generosity and grace.

"Whatever, Clay. Have your little prairie girl and someday you will see what you're missing. You'll come crawling back to me." She turns and walks away.

I'll let her think what she wants as long as she stays away from us.

Bryce and I go to the diner and get some burgers after we finish up, and it's a good attempt at a distraction—until Iris comes in.

She never told me she was working the evening shift tonight. She spots us immediately, but doesn't speak; instead, she walks behind the counter to put on her apron. Even in that old black rag, she still looks stunning. She pulls her hair up into a ponytail and smiles beautifully when Mr. and Mrs. Graff walk in.

I take a bite of my burger, hoping she'll at least acknowledge my existence, but she carries water to the table right next to us and doesn't even look my way.

"You got it bad," Bryce laughs. "She's cute and all but I don't get it."

"She's more than cute and you don't have to get it." I glare at him so that he knows he better not say another word about her.

"Alright, man, whatever makes you happy." He takes a drink of his Coke. "Hey, Iris." Bryce waves his hand and gestures her towards us.

"What the hell are you doing?" I hiss through gritted teeth.

Iris lets out a sigh and walks over to us. She puts her hands in her apron and looks at Bryce.

"Clay and I were wondering," he says with a smile, "if you'd like to join us at the movies toni—?"

"I didn't know you were working today," I interrupt. I have no idea what he's doing because we never made plans to go the movies.

"It was last-minute. There was a call-in and I had nothing better to do." She sounds emotionless.

"So... what do you say? Movies?" Bryce sounds excited. He must sense the tension and know something is going on; I know he's just trying to help. He can be a jerk eighty percent of the time, but he really is a good friend.

"Sorry, I have plans. Thanks, anyway." She smiles and walks away.

How does she have plans already? We were supposed to be hanging out tonight. I can tell she's pretty upset, but what worries me the most is that I can see in her eyes she's pulling away from me, and it scares the shit out of me. I have to talk to her. I tell Bryce I'll be right back and I follow her over to the counter. She starts rolling silverware and looks over at me.

"This isn't a good time," she says as she goes back to her work.

I put my hands together like I'm begging. "Can we talk for just a minute, please?"

She sets a stack of napkins down and walks over to me. She sounds so sweet now. "Clay, I told you that I just need a little time."

"I don't like this, Iris. I feel like I'm losing you."

I put my elbows on the counter and put my head in my hands.

"You're not losing me," she whispers, putting a comforting hand on my arm. "Just because I need time doesn't mean I want to break up."

I don't know what this girl is doing to me, but she's turning me into a big softie. I've never invested so much of myself into pleasing one person and I've certainly never shared my feelings this much. "What plans do you have?" I'm curious if she was just saying that to get out of going to the movies.

"I'm going bowling with Eric."

"Why are you hanging out with Eric?" I stand up straight.

"*Because* he's my friend and he asked if I wanted to hang out." She must not know this bothers me. Or maybe she does. She seems to do things out of spite when I mess up.

"Yeah, a friend with a major thing for you," I say. "I wish you'd just hang out with me. We could watch movies at my house."

"Clay." She shakes her head and chuckles. "That's not exactly giving me time."

"I can try." I smile. "Please be careful tonight with Eric. I don't like the way that guy looks at you."

"I will. I have to get back to work." She walks away.

I go back over to the table and sit down with Bryce. "Thanks for trying, man."

"Didn't work, huh?"

I just shake my head. We finish eating and leave, shooting Iris a wave and smile before walking out. I decide to just go home. I don't feel like hanging with anyone except her and that's not happening, so I sulk in my bedroom for the reminder of the night.

After lying here flipping through the channels for an hour, I stop on *Sweet Home Alabama* and watch it for a few minutes. It makes me think of Iris and we are similar to this movie in some ways. She's been mine all along and I've been hers.

I decide to read a little bit of the book she's writing and open it up to

Chapter Thirteen

The room is full but I feel so alone. I float through the house, retuning smiles and hugs that should comfort me but instead make me feel pitied. I can hear the voices: "that poor girl" and "what will they do without her?" Quiet whispers and unwanted glances. The table is filled with food brought from everyone who loved her but she is no longer there to enjoy it. Why is everyone smiling? Don't they feel this pain? Doesn't anyone see my mom's favorite black sweater hanging on the rack that she will never put on again? Why is her sweater still there—she's not coming back for it. I go over and take it off the hook and carry it in my arms. All of these people will leave my house and they will go on and live their lives. They will leave and I will be here, without her. My tears have dried up and I am no longer able to cry. I sink down into a corner of the couch and hold tightly onto the black sweater. It smells like her. Lily walks over and tries to take it from me.

"What are you doing?" I scream, pulling it back.

"I just want to help you." She sits down next to me. "We are all here for you."

"I don't need you." Everyone is staring now.

I bury my head in the sweater and inhale the scent of my mother.

I shut my eyes and stay like this until the whispers stop.

I feel a hand on my shoulder and it's Mayor Keller. I don't even know what he says but I stare blankly at him. Clay is by his side and he doesn't even look at me. The friend that I once had is gone, just like her. Only his departure from my life was a choice. Everyone leaves eventually. Time is a gift that we are given that leaves us with only a memory. I will no longer allow myself to be vulnerable. I will no longer welcome the new because eventually it will become the old.

Chapter Twenty

IRIS

It broke my heart to turn down Clay's invitation tonight. I wanted to give in so badly—there is no place in the world I would rather be—but I need to clear my head a bit. We've been spending so much time together that I feel like I'm losing track of who I am, the person I was before we were together. I feel like I'm opening myself up to the world, which I like, but I also feel I'm neglecting my responsibilities and the people who have always been there for me.

My conversation with Lexi was a wake-up call. I'm not too concerned about the stuff he did—it's the way she said *it won't last* that got to me the most. It made me think of who I am without him, and I couldn't find myself.

Since we've reconnected, my life has been devoted to Clay. Everything that I do, I think of him first. I don't make plans until I know that he's already busy. I love him with everything in me, however, the thought of losing that love scares me and I suppose I am preparing myself for that possibility. It's hard for me to put my trust into someone entirely, especially when it comes to my future happiness. I need to keep growing on my own so that if it doesn't work, I'm not completely broken, and can stand on my own two feet.

This is a struggle I've always faced, and as Jane Austen said: "I must learn to be content with being happier than I deserve." I'm trying, each and every day.

"See you, Tuesday, Stella." I wave as I leave the diner. Tuesday is the Fourth of July and one of our busiest days. Fortunately, everyone pitches in and works three-hour shifts so we can all enjoy the festival in town. Just in those three hours, I can make more tips than I do a whole week on my regular shift.

When I get home, Dad and the girls are sitting at the kitchen table like they've been waiting for me. I look at each of them in turn. "What's going on?"

"Sit down, honey. We all need to talk." He looks very serious.

I knew this day was coming. I knew it since the day I heard him on the phone, and seeing Mr. Keller at the farm confirmed my suspicions. My dad lost his job and we are losing the house. I sit down and am already prepared for what's coming.

"You girls already know the whole situation with the farm and why we lost it. It was a hard time for all of us, but we stuck together and we made it through, stronger than ever." He places his hand on mine and Lily's, since we are sitting next to him. "Well, Mr. Radley is getting pretty old and he doesn't have the energy to keep up with all of the upkeep and the animals. He can no longer drive the baler or do much of anything due to his knee replacement, so he's decided to sell the farm." He looks down at the table.

"Oh, Dad!" Rose cries. "Does this mean that you won't have a job anymore?"

"No, no... let me finish. These past six months, I've been trying hard to get a loan to buy the farm back. The bank turned me down, but a very generous man approached me and wants to buy the farm with me as a limited partnership." He smiles. "We're getting the farm back!"

We all jump up and hug. The farm meant so much to us all—I'd never have dreamt we'd one day have it back. Dad goes on to explain that his business partner won't be working there, but will put up the money for a fifty-fifty partnership.

"I have more great news." He smiles even bigger. "We will be returning the farm name to *Everly Place*."

Tears fill my eyes and chills run through my body. Mom chose this name when I was only three years old. I don't remember it much, but I remember the story. She and Dad were bickering in their playful way about the name; he kept coming up with the most ridiculous suggestions, but she had only one in mind. Mom told him to give it up because eventually, he would give in, and he did. He always did—he loved Mom so much that he would name the moon after her if he could.

When Mr. Radley bought the farm, he changed the name to *Radley Farms.* It was rough seeing our sign taken down and put in the shed behind our house.

"So, who is the partner?" Rose asks.

"Mr. Keller," Dad replies, and it all makes sense now.

"Maybe Clay can help bale some hay," Lily laughs.

I'm so grateful for Mr. Keller's generosity, all I can do is laugh with her. "I can't seem to picture that."

We decide to go out for ice cream and walk to Front Street Park to celebrate, so I cancel my plans with Eric and promise to visit another time.

The air refreshes us and spending time with my dad and sisters reminds me of old times. We sit under the gazebo and I'm flooded with memories. When we were kids, we would get ice cream at the local parlor often and walk to the park to watch the sunset. To this day, it's the very spot we stand and watch the tree lighting every year.

The summer before my mom passed away, she requested that we all come here every Fourth of July, because it was her favorite time of year and she was always so involved in the local Kinderfest. Seeing the kids run through the park with smiles on their faces and the sound of laughter, inflatables filling the park, and the annual Fourth of July cookout were a few of my favorite memories. That year, Dad had to push her in a wheelchair, and it took everything in her for Mom to stay seated and not get up and help out.

Lily and Rose spot an old friend who is fishing, so they go to talk to him, leaving me to chat with Dad.

"So, I assume you will need help at the farm now that you're getting it back." I take a lick of my chocolate ice cream. I'll probably have to push my plans for Bellevue out until next year, but that's OK.

"Nope." He shakes his head. "You are going to school and I'm hiring a couple high school boys to help out as needed." Dad puts his arm around me. "It's time for you to take care of yourself, young lady."

"But Dad, you need me here."

"There is a difference between need and want, Iris. I want you here, always, but I don't need you here." His words sting a little, because I always thought he needed me. "What I need is for you to make a life for yourself and to find happiness."

"I'm happy here." I smile.

"If you don't want to go to school, then that's fine. I would never force you to go. But if there is even a small part of you than wants to go and you aren't because you think I need you... then you need to go." He kisses the top of my head.

"I don't want you to be lonely, Dad." My eyes fill with tears.

"Lonely?" He laughs. "I have friends and I've actually starting seeing someone."

I jump up, astonished. "You have? Who?"

"Donna, from the bank. I took her out for dinner last week and we have plans this weekend."

I see happiness in his eyes when he says her name. A look that I haven't seen since before Mom passed. The twins and I tried to set him up on a date with our science teacher two years ago, though it didn't work out. He swore he was never dating again, but I had always hoped he would someday. He deserves to be loved.

I wrap my arms around him. "I'm so happy for you, Dad."

"See, I'll be just fine." He smiles, and I truly believe him. He *will* be just fine—and it's not forever. Leavenworth is my home, and it's where I plan to always come back to.

"OK, Dad. I'm going!" I'm beaming; it feels amazing to say it out loud. "I'm going to Bellevue," I shriek with excitement.

"Bellevue?" He looks confused. "I thought you were going to State."

"Nah, I never wanted to go there. I actually never wanted to go anywhere until recently. State is too overwhelming for me. I feel like I would be more at ease at Bellevue with the girls." My phone is buzzing in my back pocket as I explain, but I just ignore it.

"I get it. University was never my thing, either. We're a couple of introverts." He puts his arms back on the bench, and smiles back at me. "Bellevue it is."

I clap my hands together and hop up and down with excitement. I can't wait to tell Clay. I'm not sure if he will be quite as happy for me, but if he really loves me, then he will support me.

It's dark out now. We walk back to the ice cream shop where we left our vehicles when I remember to tend to my phone.

It's Clay.

What time did you plan on going bowling?

Chapter Twenty One

CLAY

I've been driving around this parking lot for a half-hour waiting for her to pull in and I haven't seen her or Eric yet. I wish she'd answer my text. I circle the parking lot one more time when she finally responds.

I didn't end up going. I spent the evening with my family instead.

Can I come see you? I ask. *I know you need space but I really want to be with you right now.*

I know I'm probably being a little pushy. She said she wanted time to think eight hours ago, and I've already seen her once in that time.

OK, come over, she relents. *I actually need to talk to you about something.*

When I walk up to the house I hear her shout from out back.

"I'm back here!"

She's in the shed pulling stuff out. "What are you doing?" I wonder.

Iris stops and looks at me, wiping her hair away from her face and smearing the dirt on her cheek. She looks like a girl on mission. "Trying to find something." She sets an old board on the ground and then tries to lift an even larger board.

"Here, let me help." I pull it out. When Iris sets her mind to something, there is nothing can stop her. I've known this since we were six and she found that nest of baby birds. She watched for two days to see if the mom came back, and when she didn't, she insisted on saving them. We brought them into the barn and she fed them three times a day—we lost one, but the ones that survived were eventually able to fly away on their own. She was so proud that day.

"Ah-ha! Here it is." She pulls out a big wooden sign.

"Hey, I remember that."

I help her finish getting it out of the shed. Once it's free, she dusts the front off with her hand and smiles.

"Everly Place, Established 2003," she reads, staring at the sign as if she's full of wonder. "I'm going to have this refinished for my dad and put on some new posts."

"Let me know what I can do to help," I tell her.

Iris puts the sign back for now and grabs her bottle of lemonade off the ground next to the shed, and we go to the side of the house to sit on the porch swing.

"I have some amazing news. My dad is getting the farm back." She lets out a whoop and the smile on her face is pure joy.

"That's awesome, Iris. I bet you are all really excited."

"Well, I guess you could say *we* are getting it back, considering it's yours just as much as it is mine."

"Huh?" I have no clue what she is talking about. How would part of her family farm be mine?

"Yeah, your dad and my dad are going to be business partners in it."

My dad doesn't ever talk to me about any of his work, so I'm clueless as to whatever's going on—but if it helps the Everlys, then I'm grateful for it. "This is news to me, but that's good, I guess."

"Good? It's amazing! Clay, my dad is getting back something he loved so much. I'm just over the moon excited for him." She wraps her arms around my neck.

Then she pulls away and looks at me, and I feel like she's not as excited to share this part. "I have more news. I'm going to Bellevue." Iris takes a sip of her lemonade and offers a smile with no emotion behind it, as if she's waiting for my reaction.

"You decided to go, huh?" I sigh and just nod my head. I'm glad she finally made a decision, because she's been dwelling on it for a while. I know I need to show my support but it's hard when I wanted her to be with me.

"I'm glad. You'll do great there. I'm happy for you, I really am." I kiss her cheek and she grins—a real one, this time.

"You are? Thank you, Clay." She lays her head on my chest. "I love you." Iris looks up and her expression is all the reassurance I needed that we are going to be OK.

"I love you, too, babe. I think this all calls for a little celebration." I pull her onto my lap.

"If only there were somewhere private we could go." She taps her finger on her chin and smiles.

"Come with me." I pull her up and we run to my truck at the end of the driveway.

"I didn't even tell my dad I was leaving."

"Iris, you're eighteen years old. He doesn't need to know every little thing you do. Unless you want to go tell him that you're leaving to get it on with your boyfriend."

She slaps my arm playfully, laughing. "Just go."

We drive out to the lake and down a two-track that is pretty grown-over, so I know that if anyone does happen to come here, they won't see us.

As soon I stop, Iris is already climbing over on my lap. Damn, she's feisty tonight. I guess I need to give her a little time more often. Her lips move slowly up and down my neck and I'm already turned on. I unbutton her jeans and she squirms to take them off, letting out a little laugh at herself. We don't have much space, so I slide my seat back as far as it will go and Iris leans back so I can unbutton my jeans. Her bare skin feels so good in my lap.

"Are you sure no one will see us?" She seems a little nervous but it isn't stopping her from wrapping her hand around me.

"No one can see us back here." I press my lips against her chest and her body feels so warm. My arms wrap around her back and slide down to caress her. I bite playfully at her arm and then ease in. She lets out a moan as she sways her hips back and forth. Her fingers run through the back of my hair and I gasp when she gives a little tug.

"Babe," she breathes and the sound of her voice arouses me even more. Her moans get louder when I grab her hips and pull her harder into me and I feel like I'm going to explode. I try and stop her for a moment and so that I can be sure that she reaches her climax before I do but she keeps going and we reach it together. She squeezes my shoulders with both hands and I gasp in delight. Her body falls weightlessly onto mine and she buries her head on my shoulder. "I love you," she whispers.

"I love you, too, so much." I kiss her shoulder and wish we that I could just hold her like this forever. I've never believed in the perfect girl—or perfect anything for that matter—but all I see in Iris is perfection, even the look she gives me she's mad and her forehead wrinkles up, the way she is always twirling her hair around her finger when she's nervous, and I especially love the way she says my name when she's being serious. I've never paid attention to such small details in a person. I run my finger over a small scar on her waist. "How'd you get that?" I ask, wanting to know every detail of her body.

She twists around to look at it. "I think I was like ten and I was running through the barn and I tripped over a bucket of grain and fell onto some chicken wire. I probably should have got stitches but my dad just glued it up and stuck a band-aid on it." She climbs off of me and moves over to the passenger side so we can get dressed.

"You did fall a lot when you were a kid," I tease her. "You were a tough girl, though. I remember when you cut your finger with a razor blade when we thought we could make pencils out of sticks." I grab her finger and look at it and see the scar. I've never noticed it until now. "You didn't even cry and I thought I was going to pass out from all the blood." We both crack up.

"I remember that. I don't know what made us think a stick could be a pencil. We never did carve down far enough to find the lead." A tear rolls down her cheek from laughing so hard, and her face is bright red. It's a perfect sound and a perfect view. If she could only see and feel what I do in this moment.

"I'm so glad we got to experience all of that together."

"Me, too." She kisses me gently and her lips feel so soft and tender.

"Alright, cowgirl, let's get you home before Daddy comes knocking on the window again." I give her a wink as she buckles her seat belt.

"Yeah, another memory for the books." She smiles and puts her hand on my leg and I take it into mine.

We get back to Iris's house, she turns towards me and asks, "Do you think I should go on birth control? We get pretty careless sometimes."

"Yeah, I think that would probably be a good idea," I tell her. I'm happy that she asked first because I was going to mention it to her.

"OK, I'll make an appointment on Monday."

"Hey, you don't still need more time, do you?"

"No." She shakes her head. "I want to spend every moment that I can with you this summer. I was just confused for a minute. Not about what you did—none of that matters, it was before us. I was just worried myself that you might get bored with me after what Lexi said." She looks down and fiddles her hair again.

"You don't ever have to worry about that. Look what we just did—you call that boring?" I laugh. "I love you, Iris. We're gonna have fun days together, exciting days, and even some lazy, boring days. I actually look forward to the lazy and boring days." I kiss her hand and smile.

"Me, too. It doesn't matter what we do; I'm always just happy to be with you," she says and I reach over and kiss her perfect lips.

Chapter Twenty Two

IRIS

I wake up Monday morning and do some chores around the house before remembering to call my doctor. I luck out, though, and they are able to work in me this afternoon.

The girls and I are going downtown later this evening to help setup for Kinderfest tomorrow. It's hard to believe it's already the Fourth of July. The summer always seems to fly by after the Fourth; it's going to be hard leaving next month, but now that it's official, I'm pretty excited to start this next chapter. I know in my heart that Clay and I will be OK—he's not only become my boyfriend, but also my best friend. My worries about Dad have also been put to rest; with the farm back and a new someone in his life, he's happier now than I've seen him in four years. He even mentioned getting back into poker night with some old friends. There is nothing holding me back, and I'm ready to spread my wings.

When I arrive at the doctor's office, I have to fill out a whole book of paperwork—and since I now fall into the "sexually active" category, I get to have my very first Pap smear. I'm not too thrilled about that. I begin to feel nauseated, and I know it's because my nerves are so high right now. I've had the same family doctor since I was a baby, and now I have to go in and tell her that I'm having sex and need birth control.

The exam portion of the appointment isn't quite as bad as I anticipated. It's uncomfortable, but quick. We go over birth control options and decide to go with the Pill for now.

"We'll need to do a pregnancy test before I write up your prescription. It's just standard protocol," Dr. Ramsey explains.

After I've given my sample, I sit back in the exam room and wait for the doctor to come back. I get a text from Clay asking if I'd like to go to a cookout with him this evening at his grandparents' house, but I have to decline, since the twins and I already committed to setting up inflatables for the festival. I tell him all about my unpleasant exam and that I'll be on birth control by the end of the night. We agree to meet up tomorrow for the pancake breakfast at the American Legion. I'm looking forward to spending the whole day with him tomorrow and watching fireworks over the lake tomorrow night.

Dr. Ramsey returns and I stick my phone under my leg. "Iris, what was the first date of your last menstrual cycle?" she asks.

I'm not sure. I pull out my phone to consult my calendar. "I can't remember the exact date, but it was sometime at the end of May."

"Well, we won't be starting you on birth control right now because your pregnancy test came back positive." She places her hand on my shoulder and I am speechless. "You're pregnant, Iris."

"Pregnant?" I spit out.

"Yes. How do you feel about this?"

"I'm pregnant?" I ask again.

"You are. We'll need to setup an ultrasound to determine exactly how far along, but I assume you are no more than five weeks pregnant. Are you OK, Iris?"

"No, no, I'm not OK. I can't be." I start crying. "I'm only eighteen. How can this be? I've only had unprotected sex a couple of times." I bury my face in my hands, wondering how I will ever tell Clay, or Dad.

"My dad is going to kill me," I blurt as I'm sobbing. "And... I drank alcohol last week." How can this be happening? I can't take care of a baby. I have my whole life ahead of me. I was finally in a good place and decided to go to college. Clay and I are enjoying our very new relationship.

"Many women drink before finding out they are pregnant and the baby is just fine. You have nothing to worry about. As long as you don't consume any alcohol or drugs from this point forward, there is no reason to doubt you will have a healthy pregnancy," she assures me.

"OK." I wipe my tears. "So, what's next?"

Dr. Ramsey hands me a pamphlet, "Here is some information on your options."

I immediately notice the words abortion and adoption and hand it back to her. "Abortion and adoption are not an option."

"OK, that's your decision. You'll need to go to the lab next door and we'll do a blood draw just to check your hCG and progesterone levels. That will confirm the pregnancy. Rhonda at the front desk will get you set up for your ultrasound and I'll send in a prescription for your prenatal vitamins. Everything will be OK, Iris." She tries to comfort me again.

I leave the office and Rhonda tells me that she will call me Wednesday morning with the date and time for my ultrasound. The lab is in the same building, so I get my draw, and they tell me I should get a call with the results later today.

I slide into the seat of my car and sit in silence for what feels like forever. I'm trying to wrap my mind around all of this and I feel overwhelmed and sick again. I finally pull myself together enough to drive home.

Rose is sitting in the living room when I walk in the door and I try to hold it together but I can't. As soon as she looks at me, I break down and cry. She rushes over to my side as we sink down to the floor and she sits there, holding me.

"Iris, what happened? What's going on?" She sounds so worried.

"Rose... I'm... I'm pregnant." I finally get it out.

Her face is pale and she is in just as much shock as I am. Lily walks in and hurries over to us and Rose repeats what I just told her.

"How am I going to take care of a baby?" I start sobbing again.

They both comfort me and try to reassure me that everything will be OK. I make them promise not tell anyone—especially Dad—for now.

The girls take a ride to the pharmacy and get my vitamins for me and bring me back some soup and a sandwich for dinner.

A few hours later, I get a call from the doctor's office confirming that I am, in fact, pregnant.

I spend the rest of the night watching sappy movies in bed and crying my eyes out. I feel awful that I bailed on Dad and the girls with the festival setup, but they will have plenty of helping hands. There is no way I would be able to hold it together. As I'm lying in bed caught up in a movie, it slips my mind for a moment, until a rush comes over and I hear Dr. Ramsey's words replay in mind: my test was positive and I'm pregnant.

I place my hand on my stomach for a second. I feel a sense of love for the life growing inside of me. I pull out my phone and Google information on pregnancy and find a site that tells me that at five weeks, the baby is the size of an apple seed.

I smile with a newfound realization that everything will be OK. I just have to tell Clay.

Chapter Twenty Three

CLAY

The visit with my grandparents was nice, but I'm glad they didn't mind when I left a little early. I couldn't stand to sit there with Luke much longer; the tension between us is at an all-time high and I'm sick of everyone trying to meddle in it. Besides, I'm excited to surprise Iris and help her with the festival preparations.

"Hey, Mr. Everly." I extend my hand and he returns with a shake. "Have you seen Iris around?"

"Hi, Clay. No, she wasn't feeling well, so she stayed home," he says as he lifts a pole to a canopy.

"Here, let me help with that." I hold the pole while he adjusts the straps. "She's not feeling well, huh? She never mentioned anything."

"Yeah, some stomach bug or something. Hopefully, with some rest, she'll be feeling better by tomorrow. I know she'd be bummed if she had to miss everything."

"Yeah, for sure. I'm gonna go text her. Do you got all this OK?" I point to the canopy.

"Oh, yeah, I've done it every year. Thanks, Clay." He smiles. I move to my phone.

How are you feeling, babe?

I'm relieved when she responds: *A little bit better but still under the weather.*

I left my grandparents' early, I offer. *Want me to come keep you company?*

I'm actually really tired. I think I might just go to bed.

Is everything else OK?

Of course, it's just been a long day. I'll see you in the morning?

Definitely. Feel better. Love you.

I love you, too.

I notice Mr. Everly struggling a bit, so I help him finish setting up and then walk down to the Arts and Crafts Fair to see if Mom made it there yet.

"Keller!" I hear Bryce's voice.

I turn around and see Bryce and a few of our friends, along with Lexi. I turn back and keep walking. Damn him, he knows I can't stand to be around that girl.

"Yo, wait up." He catches up to me.

"What the hell is she doing with you guys?"

"I don't know, she's just tagging along. I think her and Liam have something going on. Come with us."

"Hell no, I'm not going anywhere with her." I grit my teeth; he should know this.

"Just ignore her. We're having a bonfire at the lake and I got a nice selection of fireworks." He tries to sound convincing.

"I can't, man." We're still walking because I know if I stop, the group will catch up to us.

"Come on, ever since you started dating that girl you skip out on everything."

"That girl has a name."

"OK—*Iris*—has you wrapped around her finger. Lighten up and let's go."

"She does not. I'm not even seeing her tonight, but if she knew I was hanging around Lexi, she would be pissed."

"So, we'll ditch her." He laughs. "Come on, we got a case of beer. It's summer break." He's practically begging now.

"Alright, one beer." I'm not in the mood, but if I don't give in, he will follow me all night. "I'll meet ya there."

I pull down the two-track until Bryce's car is in front of me. Liam is starting a fire, and Lexi and Kate are trying to put on music in Liam's truck. I'm glad she found a different guy to obsess over until she cheats on him and moves onto the next. I can't believe I was ever into that girl.

"Where's your girlfriend?"

Damnit, I thought I could get through this night without talking to her.

"She's sick." I stare straight ahead without looking at Lexi. I'm trying to be nice, but if she pushes my buttons, I have no problem telling her off.

"Aww, poor girl." It's sarcastic.

"What do you want, Lexi?"

She frowns and inches too close for my comfort. "I'm just making conversation. We're still friends, aren't we?"

"No, Lexi, we're not friends."

"Geez, rude much?" She swings her head and slaps me with her hair.

I should be with Iris right now. I should be making her soup and rubbing her back, trying to help her feel better. I pull out my phone to text her goodnight and Bryce throws me a beer at the same time; I jump back to try and catch it but miss, and drop my phone and my beer at the same time.

"Dude, terrible catch." Bryce laughs.

"I wasn't looking, dickhead." I grab my beer but I can't find my phone anywhere. It's dark now and I can't see a damn thing. "Let me see your cell flashlight."

Bryce and I look for a good twenty minutes before I find it sitting on a big branch. It seems odd that it would land on a branch, but I don't think much of it.

I hope you're feeling better. I just wanted to tell you goodnight.

I hit send and stick my phone in the pocket of my jeans.

"So, fireworks at my cabin tomorrow night? You'll be there, right?" Bryce asks.

"No, man, not this year, sorry."

"Clay, we've gone to the cabin every year since we were fifteen. Everyone goes. What the hell."

"I'm watching the fireworks with Iris at the park," I tell him.

"It's like I said earlier: that girl's got you whipped." He shakes his head.

"If you ever had a serious relationship you would understand but you haven't, so back off."

My phone beeps. Iris.

Why would you send me that?

Send you what? I wonder.

Those pictures of Lexi and her friends?

I scroll through our previous texts, baffled, but there are no pictures. All I can say is: *I have no idea what you're talking about.*

Where are you? Iris wants to know.

At the lake.

Is Lexi there?

She is, I admit, *but I'm not hanging out with her. She's here with Liam.*

Well, you either sent me pictures of her or she did and if it wasn't you then why the hell did she have your phone?

"Lexi! What the hell did you do?" I shout, and everyone looks at me.

She laughs. "Chill out. It was just a joke."

"Fuck!" I yell. "I told you to stay the hell away from me and Iris and you take my phone and send her pictures. What the hell is wrong with you?"

But I'm too busy right now to keep yelling. I have to let Iris know what happened; I can't let her sit there, sick and hurt and thinking I'm partying with my ex. *I lost my phone and she must have grabbed it. I swear, babe.*

OK, she says, and that's all. *We will talk tomorrow. I'm going back to bed. Have fun with Lexi tonight.*

She always does that. She always has to throw in that last punch.

I'm not with Lexi. I'm with my friends and Lexi happens to be here. I try to avoid her but it's a small town, sometimes she is gonna pop up places.

She doesn't respond. I know I should go to her but she needs rest, and if I go, we will be up all night arguing and making up, so I decide against it. I wish she wouldn't worry about Lexi, but after reading her book I'm starting to understand more about her insecurities. It's not so much Lexi or any other girl she's worried about; she's worried about losing me.

"I'm out." I throw my can into a pile and give a wave over my shoulder as I walk to my truck.

"One more, Keller. Come on," Bryce sighs.

"Nope, I said one." I climb in my truck and get the hell out of there.

In the past, I would have given in. I've always been a people-pleaser. I always tried to make everyone around me laugh. If I was dared to do something, I was never asked twice; I did it. Lately, I'm starting to see the bigger picture. Most of the people I call friends won't even be in my life five years from now. I'm starting to care less about impressing everyone else and focusing more on my life and my future. Bryce is my best friend and I'll always be cool with him, and I've got a network of good people, but sometimes you really do have to lose to gain; it comes with the changes in life.

When I get home, I open up Iris's book and pick up where I left off.

It's been one week since I lost her. I went to school today and apparently Dad set it up so that I would talk to Ms. White, the school counselor.

She talked to me about the different stages of grieving and I don't believe any of it. I believe that we all grieve in our own way and in our own time. There is no instruction manual that tells you how to get over the loss of someone you love. I made it through the first week, and I'll make it through the second, and the third. I'll make it but I'll never get over it. I'll never stop missing her. I'll always love Mom. I just wish my love could bring her back.

Chapter Twenty Four

IRIS

I know he's right. Lexi is going to be around.

She's a part of his group of friends, and I have to accept that. I do not have to accept her disrespect for our relationship, though, and if she continues these antics to try and rouse my suspicions toward Clay, then I have no problem telling her exactly how I feel. I'm not playing into her foolish games any longer; I have more important things to focus on, like making sure I am healthy mentally and physically for my baby. Lexi is just an added stressor that I don't need.

I flip off the light switch on my nightstand and try and sleep, but my mind plays out the conversation I have to have with Clay tomorrow, over and over and over.

Morning finally comes, and I feel like I haven't slept at all. I drag myself out of bed and prepare for the busy day ahead. I am still having moments if nausea, but it seems to come and go. The aroma of coffee inundates the house and it's a familiar scent that hasn't filled my senses in years. Mom drank coffee religiously, but Dad never took to it.

I enter the kitchen and see a lady with curly brunette hair facing away from me. She turns her head and I realize it's Donna.

"Iris, good morning. Your dad just stepped out for a minute." She sips on her coffee. I notice Mom's old coffee pot on the counter, and it looks like it was partially dusted off. She'd be pleased it's getting use and I know she would be happy for Dad. The scene brings a calm to me I haven't felt in a very long time. I'm grateful that this woman woke the happiness that has been sleeping in him for so long.

"Oh, OK. Are you and my dad going to down to the Legion this morning?" Every Fourth of July, the American Legion holds a big pancake breakfast to kick off the day, and the whole town attends.

"Yes, will you be joining us?"

"Yep. I'll be meeting my boyfriend there in an hour." I smile and take a seat.

I keep Donna company while Dad is out. Apparently, he had to run over and fix something in the barn. When he returns, they leave, and I take a quick shower and throw on a red, white, and blue dress—the same one I've worn today for the last three years. I put a single braid in my hair and send Clay a quick text to let him know I'm on my way.

The tables are all lined up in rows and a buffet of pancakes and other sides teem up front. I spot Clay sitting with his parents and an empty seat next him. I make my way through the maze of people and finally reach them.

"Hey, there. I saved you a seat," Clay says as he pulls out my chair.

My nerves are getting the best of me right now, knowing that when we leave here, I have to tell Clay I'm pregnant. I'm suddenly not feeling very hungry but I force myself to eat a little bit. His dad talks about the farm and how happy he is to be doing this partnership with my dad. I thank him for his kindness and for giving my dad back something that meant so much to him.

When we finish, I ask Clay if we can go for a walk, because there is something I need to tell him. I'm unsure how he's going to react. I imagine he will be shocked just like I was—then scared—and then hopefully, at some point, we can both accept this and find happiness.

"I've missed you." He takes my hand into his and reaches over, kissing my cheek. "I'm glad you're feeling better. I know today is important to you and you would have been bummed if you had to miss all the fun."

"I've missed you, too." I smile at him. "Let's sit here."

We stop at a bench at the entrance to the park. It's already flooded with people and kids running all around. The smiles on the children's faces warm my heart and bring a smile to my own.

"So, what's going on? Is everything OK?" Clay asks.

I'm not sure exactly where to begin. I wonder for a moment if I should start with the beginning of my appointment and tell him how everything happened step-by-step, or just jump right in and tell him I'm pregnant.

"You're shaking." He places his hands over mine. "Just tell me what's wrong." He is serious now, and I think he knows this is more than a conversation about school or Lexi.

"I don't know how to say this, Clay." Tears begin to pool in my eyes.

He's worried now. "Just say it."

"Yesterday... at the doctor." I pause.

His eyes widen. "What happened?"

"She told me that I'm pregnant." I said it—my heart is racing and my palms are sweaty.

Clay pulls his hands away from mine and turns straight ahead. He's silent and stares at a black lab on a leash in front of us, like he's trying to distract himself from his thoughts.

"I'm pregnant, Clay. Say something, please, anything," I beg of him.

"No! You can't be." He sounds angry or confused—I can't tell which it is.

"I most definitely am. I'm not sure how far yet but I'll have an ultrasound next week sometime."

"You can't keep it." He stands.

"What?" I stand up with him. "What do you mean *I* can't keep it? What are you suggesting?" I cross my arms and feel anger building up inside of me. If he's suggesting what I think he is than he's not the man I thought I knew.

"Iris." He puts his hands on my arms. "I'm only nineteen years old. I can't have a baby. We have our whole lives ahead of us. Think about this, Iris. We have options."

I shake his hands off of me. "Are you asking me to get an abortion?" Just saying the word makes me feel sick. "I would never!" I shout and then remember that we are in a crowded public place.

"My dad will kill me. I'm already on my last straw with him."

"This isn't about your dad. This is about us and our baby." I can't believe he is saying these things. I knew he might have a hard time at first, maybe be a little upset, but I never contemplated him wanting an abortion. "I'm not doing it, Clay, and nothing will change my mind. I'm having a baby whether you like it or not and if you can't accept that then I'll raise it by myself." I huff and walk away as fast as I can before I make a scene.

Clay doesn't come after me. Three hours pass, and he hasn't called, texted, or tried to find me. I'm still hopeful that once he's had time to process all of this, he will change his mind. I won't allow this to ruin my day. The Fourth is special. Clay will come around.

My short and busy shift at the diner flies. Happy to be out of there—so I can try and salvage the rest of the day—I wander around for a bit, looking for my sisters and dad. While strolling through the Arts and Crafts Fair, I come across an adorable pair of yellow crochet baby booties; I buy them quickly before anyone notices and ask for a bag to put them in.

I find Dad down at the lake by the park, where the fishing contest has begun. Another festival tradition we've always taken part in—Dad has never won, but he still tries every year. It's a time for him to be social and crack jokes with the townsfolk. All the fish are weighed and then tossed back. Dad has actually landed the smallest fish before, but there is no prize for smallest.

He used to take us fishing often when we were kids. Lily and Rose wouldn't touch the bait or the fish, but always I preferred to unhook my own; it's part of the glory of a good catch.

The rest of the day is spent walking around the Arts and Crafts Fair with my sisters and Amber. I ran into Mr. Bonn, who owns a wood restoration business, and he happily agrees to refinish the old farm sign for me. Before long, it's six o'clock, and we head to the BBQ picnic in the park.

It's been eight hours since I've talked to Clay, and I'm starting to miss him. I've really been looking forward to watching the fireworks with him, but now I'm worried it may not happen, at all.

Chapter Twenty Five

CLAY

"Toss me another one," I yell to Bryce as I chuck my finished beer can to the side. The cabin is quiet and peaceful right now; everyone is in town.

Bryce's family cabin sits directly across the lake from the festival, close enough to see the fireworks. We've been coming here on the Fourth for years. When we were younger, we'd come with Bryce's parents, but they stopped tagging along while we've made it a tradition. Once the festival calms down, most of our friends will be headed out here to party for the night.

The beer is helping to drown out the noise in my head, but if I keep going at this pace, I may not make it until sundown. Iris hasn't tried to call me at all. I'm sure she's pissed off at me and I don't blame her; I was an ass. I'm not ready for a baby, but I wouldn't want her to have an abortion. I don't even know why I said that—it was just a reaction. I'm not ready to tell her yet, though. I need to clear my head and think through my next step before I can even be around her. She's got a lot going on emotionally, too, and I need to be able to be strong for her. And for our baby.

I put my head back on the reclining air chair and shut my eyes behind my sunglasses. I can see Iris's long blonde hair. She smiles and turns her head, and the wind blows her hair, and as I brush it off from her face, I press my lips against hers. I can still taste the lemonade on her lips from our last kiss. My heart races as I think about the feeling of her arms around my neck and mine around her waist. When she's in my arms, I feel like I am keeping her safe. I always want to protect her—not just physically, but emotionally, too. Maybe I am the one she needs emotional protection from, though. I always seem to put my foot in my mouth and hurt her.

Bryce walks over and pushes my chair back and I tip all the way into the ground. He and Liam laugh hysterically as I stand up and brush myself off. "Hey, fucker, I almost spilled my beer."

"Dude, you need to lighten up. What's that girl done to you this time?" Bryce asks, still laughing.

"I told you to quit calling her *that girl,* and she didn't do anything. I'm the one who screwed up," I huff and then pick up the chair to sit back down.

"Oh, shit, what'd you do? You fucked Lexi, didn't you?" Bryce asks and Liam's eyes get wide.

"Hell no! Just drop it, man. I need another beer." I make my way over to the cooler, crack one open, and sit back down in my chair overlooking the lake.

"Alright, alright. I'm gonna start grilling burgers." Bryce pats my back and walks away.

Knowing that Iris is directly across the lake from me is torture. I was really looking forward to spending the evening together and hoped I could even convince her to come back to the cabin and stay the night with me. I wonder what she's doing at this very moment. She's probably laughing with her family and showing those gorgeous dimples of hers.

I stand up and walk closer to the lake, taking a drink of my beer. A light gust of wind shakes the leaves over my head. I walk out into the dock and stare aimlessly in the direction of the festival. The lake is large, so I can't see anything, but I know the vicinity. My heart longs for the girl—the woman—that I love. The woman that is carrying my unborn child. I contemplate all the different ways I could tell my parents that Iris and I are having a baby, and I can't seem to come up with the right combination of words that end with them accepting this, especially my father.

I turn around when I hear a few vehicles pull in. The sun is starting to set now and it won't be long until the fireworks start. I send Iris a quick message just to let her know that I love her and to think of me when she's watching tonight. She doesn't respond, so I stick my phone back into the pocket of my jeans.

Bryce finishes up the grilling, and I'm standing over a table of burgers and chips but not feeling much like eating, so I grab another beer, instead.

"Take a swig of this." Liam passes me a bottle of vodka. I take a big gulp and chase it down with my beer.

Vehicles are piling in now and the party is getting started. I'm feeling good and letting loose—it's been awhile since I've had a carefree night and tonight that is exactly what I plan to have. The fire blazes in the fire pit and Bryce and I start lighting off some fireworks by the lake. We set off a bottle rocket that goes astray and shoots into the crowd. The girls are squirming and the guys are cracking up.

The music is turned up and the sun is going down. I glance around the party to see who is here now, and I catch Lexi looking at me. She smiles but I turn my head. I don't want to be a dick to her, but if I return the smile, I know she'll come talk to me, and I don't need that shit right now. I can't put it past her to try and start another war.

My dismissal of her smile wasn't good enough, because I look to my left, and she's walking towards me.

"Hi Clay." She smiles.

I don't say a word but instead turn towards the lake in hopes of her just going away.

"Look, I know you don't want to talk to me, but I want to apologize for how I've been behaving."

"Got it. Thanks," I say without looking at her.

"I mean it, Clay. I apologized to Iris today, too. It's just hard for me knowing how bad I messed up and then seeing you with her—it was too much for me. But I'm over it."

"You've seen Iris? What did you say to her?" I spin around and feel anger rising. She better not have tried to start problems.

"I apologized for the picture incident and told her that I hope you two are happy. Calm down, Clay, I'm not a monster." She places her hand in my arm but I shake it away. "She looked happy... she was with Amber, oh, and that Eric kid."

"Eric, huh?"

"Yep. I don't mean to start problems but they looked pretty cozy on the park bench. He had his arm around her." Lexi pauses as she examines my reaction, but her smirk suggests she knows exactly what she's doing. "Anyway, I just wanted to apologize. Enjoy the party."

She spins and walks away and leaves me here with more questions, but none that I want her to answer, because then she will see my suspicions.

Iris and Eric? I should be glad that she's happy, but why is she with him? I can't help but wonder if part of her is missing me at all right now. She's with him; she's not coming back to me. I pushed her away by telling her I didn't want our baby. The image of she and Eric and laughing and him touching her sends me back over to the bottle of liquor that I swig until the burn is replaced with emptiness.

Chapter Twenty Six

IRIS

"I knew that he would be upset," I tell Lily, "but I didn't think he'd tell me to get rid of it." I bury my face in my hands and try to hide my tears. Eric makes his way back over to us, so I wipe them away, and smile.

"OK, I'm ready," he says with a blanket in his hands. Lily and Rose are heading to a party at a cabin with some friends, so I'm watching the fireworks with Eric at the park.

"See you at home." I smile and wave goodbye to the twins.

The park is crowded with chairs, blankets, and standing people. We find a spot under a tree and Eric lays down the blanket.

"Thanks for watching with me," I say as I pull on my sweater and sit down. "If you hadn't, then I'd likely be watching them alone." I laugh, but it isn't really funny. It's kind of embarrassing that everyone I know is busy and that I've never made an attempt to make more friends.

"I wouldn't want to be watching them with anyone else." He lies down on his side, facing me with his fist under his cheek. "Unless you want to go to Bryce Thomas's party at his cabin. Everyone is going."

"No, I think I'll probably just go home after fireworks. It's been a long day."

I imagine that Clay is probably at Bryce's and even though I miss him, I don't feel like talking to him if he's drinking, and I'm sure he is. I still haven't responded to his text.

Eric keeps nonchalantly moving closer and closer, and I hope that he isn't getting the wrong idea. I've led him on before, and that's not my intention tonight. He's a good friend, and I'm happy he is here, but he will never be anything more than that.

"They're starting." I point the sky.

We *ooh* and *ahh* over show. The grand finale rains beautiful exploding colors throughout the sky. Then I feel Eric's hand on my shoulder, and I turn to look at him, and he's moving towards me and before I have a second to think, his lips are pressed to mine.

I push him away. "Why did you do that?" I sound harsh, but I don't mean to. "You know I have a boyfriend."

He looks surprised. "I know you did, but I figured if you weren't with him tonight, then maybe you two broke up and when I saw you crying earlier, I assumed it was because he did something to hurt you."

"No, we didn't break up. We just had a disagreement. Look, Eric, I'm sorry if I led you on, but you and I are nothing more than friends." My voice is lower now, but he still looks hurt and embarrassed.

"OK, I'm good with being friends. But if Clay ever screws up, you know how I feel. Until then, friends is good." He smiles.

This was a little awkward, but at least we have an understanding now. The grand finale finishes and we all clap. I grab my phone off the blanket before standing and up and see two messages from Lily.

One: *Have you talked to Clay at all? He's pretty wasted.*

Two: *Some girl keeps hanging all over him.*

"Do you still wanna go to the party at the cabin?" I ask Eric as I begin to shake off the blanket and fold it up. "I'll drive."

"Um... sure."

Jealousy kicks in, and even though Clay and I are in a bad spot right now, I need to make sure he doesn't do anything that could destroy our relationship for good. My heart is racing and the idea of having a civil conversation seems far-fetched, but I have to see him.

It's about a twenty-minute drive to the other side of the lake and Eric directs me where to go. We pull down a long dirt road lined with elegant Victorian houses, then turn down an even longer dirt road until reaching Bryce's family cabin where it sits at the end, overlooking the lake. There are at least twenty cars here and I can hear the music before even getting out of mine.

I spot my sisters immediately. Rose has her arms thrown around a guy's neck, the same guy from the bonfire. They must have a little fling going on, but she's never mentioned it; she's always been quite private when it comes to relationships with men.

My eyes scan from person to person until I spot Clay staggering around a cooler with sunglasses on. Sunglasses at night—he is definitely intoxicated. I watch as a tall, thin brunette who I've never seen before pulls on his arm, laughing, and he follows. He sits down on a chair and she plops her drunk self into his lap. He seems oblivious as to what is going on around him, but he goes with it.

"I'll be right back," I tell Eric, leaving him standing alone.

I walk through the crowd and finally reach Clay. The brunette has her arms around his neck now and is whispering something in his ear when he laughs. I stand directly in front of him with my arms crossed.

"Can I help you?" The brunette turns around. I'm not sure if it's my hormones or the situation, but I have no filter at this point.

Clay just sits there like he isn't the least bit fazed by my presence.

"Yes, you could get off my boyfriend's lap." I gesture my hands towards Clay.

"This guy claims he's single so I think you need to get lost." She rolls her eyes.

"I said get the hell off my boyfriend's lap. He's obviously drunk and doesn't know what the hell he's doing," I shout. It's taking everything in me not to grab her by her hair and pull her off. I've never been the possessive type, but this isn't settling well with me. If I weren't pregnant, I probably would've made a scene by now.

"Clay." I kneel down so I'm next to his face, ignoring the wench sitting on him. "Get up, we need to talk." I pull his arm.

"Hey, Iris! Happy Fourth of July." He takes off his sunglasses and smiles. "This is my friend, Tammy."

"It's Tanya," she corrects him.

"Same thing."

"Clay, get up." I pull his arm again.

"I don't think I can. There's a chick sitting on my lap." His eyes wander from me to her and the casualness in his tone is insulting.

"I'm trying really hard to be nice here, Clay. Will you please get up and come talk to me?"

"You OK, Iris?" Eric is standing next to us now.

"Yeah, I'm..."

"Eric!" Clay shouts. "How nice of you to join us. Did you and her come together?" He points to me with a sour look on his face.

Eric nods. He can see Clay is wasted and the girl who is still in his lap probably tells him that I'm not very happy right now. "Come on, Iris. You don't need to deal with this asshole right now."

Clay starts to stand up and the girl slides off his lap and onto the ground, laughing. He's having a little trouble, so I extend my hand, and he takes it until he's finally on two feet.

"Are you trying to take my girl?" Clay gets in Eric's face.

This isn't going to go well. I pull him back by his shirt. "Clay, stop it."

"You're drunk," Eric spits and Clay gives him a very hard shove that sends him stumbling backwards.

"I see what you're doing. You're trying to move in and take her from me." He pushes Eric again.

I stay back because I can't be in the middle of this, but I yell for Clay to stop repeatedly.

"Rose," I yell as she walks by, "stop him." She knows that I'm pregnant and can't help, so she rushes over and pulls Clay away from Eric who is now pissed and screaming in his face.

"It's best if we leave," I tell Rose and she nods in agreement.

I realize now that coming here was a big mistake. I walk over to Eric and brush him off and apologize, but he assures me it's not my fault.

"If you leave with him, we're over," Clay shouts and at this point I don't even care, I just need to get out of here.

I take Eric's arm and walk away, giving Clay one last look and behind the bloodshot, blank stare, I see sadness and it breaks my heart, but I keep walking. Rose holds onto him until we are out of sight.

Chapter Twenty Seven

CLAY

When I wake up Wednesday morning, the sun is beaming down and I'm drenched in sweat. I peel myself off the lounge chair I must have passed out in and kick a few cans away from me. Everything is quiet and still, besides the embers crackling in the fire pit. Beer cans fill the perfectly landscaped yard. The sliding door to the cabin is open. I open a couple coolers in search of a bottled water with no luck. When I walk into the cabin, I notice a couple people on the floor under a blanket, and Liam on the couch.

I search the cupboards until I find a cup and fill it with cold water. It tastes so refreshing, and I refill and slam another glass. Bryce walks in with his hand on head.

"I feel ya, bro," I say to him. We walk back outside with a couple trash bags and begin picking up the scattered trash.

"You were pretty messed up last night," Bryce chuckles. "I couldn't believe you went off on Eric Somers, of all people."

"What? Oh, hell." I don't remember any of this. I don't even recall seeing Eric last night. I drop the bag and sit down on a wooden chair. "What happened?"

"Eric and Iris showed up and you were all over some girl. Apparently, you shoved Eric and few times and then dumped Iris before she left." He sits down next to me. "I didn't see any of it, but I heard all about it."

"Fuck!" I slam my fist into the table.

I pull out my phone and have no messages or missed calls. I must have really done it this time. I put my head in my hands trying to remember, but my mind is blank.

"I broke up with, Iris?" My head is hanging down as if by a thread.

"I guess so. She left with Eric and you were pretty pissed," he offers as he continues to pick up cans.

"I hate to bail on you, man, but I gotta go."

"Alright, call me later. Let me know how it goes."

It's eleven a.m., and Iris should be home. Instead of calling her, I head straight to her house. I have to find out what happened and I have to make it right. But I reek of alcohol and decide that I better swing home and clean up first—the smell on my breath and clothes may disgust her and remind her of my reckless behavior last night.

I feel a mound of regrets and the sun is burning my eyes but I can't seem to find my sunglasses anywhere. It all sounds bad, really bad. Iris must be so hurt by this. If only I hadn't been a jerk when she told me she was pregnant. I should have been more careful and used protection and we wouldn't even be in this mess.

Luke is on the couch when I get home, and Mom is out back doing some gardening. After I shower and get dressed, I feel a little better, but my head is still pounding and my stomach is still in knots from regret.

"Hi, honey." Mom walks into the kitchen. "How was your stay at the cabin?"

She moves to the sink and washes the dirt off her hands. Mom knows that I usually stay at the Thomas cabin on the Fourth; she just doesn't know what all that entails.

"Uneventful," I lie.

"Your dad and I were planning to take the boat out this weekend and we'd really like if you and Iris would come."

"We can probably do that. I'll talk to Iris." I grab a water and a Pop-Tart. "I'm going to see her now. I'll be home later." I kiss her cheek.

Mom is so kind and innocent that I don't dare mention any of my problems to her. If she only knew half of the shit I've done, she'd disown me. I still don't know how I'll tell her about the baby. After I talk to Iris, I'll figure it out. I know I have to start taking some responsibility for my actions.

When I pull into the Everly driveway, I notice that Iris's car isn't here. I try and call her but it doesn't even ring; it just goes to voicemail. I go down to the diner, figuring she might be at work. I don't see her car, but she could still be here, so I go in.

The diner is pretty busy today. I wave to a group of friends I went to school with whom I remember being at the party last night.

"Keller!" They call me over.

I let out a sigh and go over, remembering the fresh shame I feel inside. I stick my hands in my short pockets. "How's it going?"

"That was quite a party last night," Mike says. "I'm still feeling like shit today."

"Yeah, no kidding." I glance around for Iris.

"That girl you were with was pretty hot. Is she local?" another guy says.

"I don't even know her, man."

They all laugh. I wish I could remember the night but I don't want to remember her. She will just be a constant reminder of my screw up.

"Nice," Mike says. "That must have been pretty strange for her, waking up on a chair with a guy she doesn't even know." They laugh again.

Shit, she fell asleep on the chair with me. She must have snuck off before I woke up. I don't know how I'm going to explain any of this to Iris.

"I gotta go. I'll see you guys around." I smile and wave as I walk away.

"Stella, is Iris working today?" I ask one of the waitresses I recognize.

She shrugs and continues to her table with a tray of food. "No, Clay. She had something come up and will be off for the rest of the week."

I'm starting to get concerned. Iris wouldn't take time off from work unless it was serious. I have to find her. I try calling her a couple times, but it goes straight to voicemail.

I figure I'll go by her house one more time and see if anyone knows where she might be. At last resort, I'll call Eric. I owe him an apology, anyways.

This time, when I get to the Everlys', her sisters' car is here, so I knock on the door. Lily opens it and walks out, closing it behind her.

"You have some nerve, coming here." She looks angry and I back up a little bit.

"I'm just trying to find Iris. I need to talk to her."

She crosses her arms. "Iris doesn't want to talk to you, so just stay away from her."

I know I messed up, but was it really bad enough for her sister to think I need to stay away from her? I throw my head back and beg her to tell me where she is. But she doesn't budge.

"Lily, I love your sister and I need to explain to her how sorry I am. Please, just tell me where she is." I feel the depression from the alcohol and the pain of hurting Iris and I lose control as tears fill my eyes. "Please, I'm begging you."

Lily stands there, silently observing me, and I think she realizes how remorseful I am. The sun is hidden behind the clouds now and I feel a dread overcome me. I've never been this serious about someone, and I can't lose her. The thought of Iris not being in my life makes me feel ill and empty.

"Clay, she left." She uncrosses her arms and sits on the porch step.

"Left where?" I sit next down next to her and put my face in my hands as I blink away the tears.

"I can't tell you that. She needed to get away for a little bit." She looks at me. "She lost the baby, Clay."

Chapter Twenty Eight

IRIS

"Hi, Mom. It's Iris."

I lay my head down on the ground next to the tomb that reads *Beloved Mother and Wife*.

"I really miss you. Why did you leave me? Why does everyone always leave me?" Beads of water begin falling one after another. I trace my fingers over her name on the cement block that is supposed to bring people remembrance and peace, but fills me with sadness. My legs curl up to my chest, and I stay still for what feels like hours. It's so quiet and calm and I feel closer to her here. For years after her death, I would often write Mom letters and bury them here next to her; I used to think she would read them. There are probably a dozen letters underneath this dirt I lie on.

The day we buried Mom, I wanted to climb in that hole with her. I didn't know how I was going to live without her here. Now I have to live with that same loss of my own unborn child.

I never met him or her, but I loved my baby. The loss isn't the same, but the emptiness I feel is.

Last night, I came home and went to bed feeling fine. I woke up in the middle of the night with bad cramping and when I went into the bathroom, the blood kept coming. I lay down until morning with no sleep until the doctor's office opened. They got me in right away, and after the blood work showed that my levels had dropped significantly, they confirmed what I already knew.

I blamed Clay for a minute. Then I blamed myself, because I drank before I knew, but Dr. Ramsey assured me that nothing could be done to prevent this, and that sometimes there is just an issue with implantation and other factors beyond control.

I peel myself off the ground and sit up. My eyes are puffy and my hair is knotted. I am wearing the same sweatpants I wore to bed and a black T-shirt; I notice only now it says *Love Life*. Right now, I'm having a hard time loving myself, let alone life.

I'm still in an immense amount of pain, but the Motrin is helping. I pick up my keys and my phone, which has been turned off, and I blow a kiss to Mom before going to my car and heading to Seattle.

I turn on the radio as I'm driving, and it seems like every song is speaking to me. I can't hold back the tears, so I let them continue to fall off my cheek and onto my sweatpants. My window is all the way down and the air feels nice against my arm as I hang my hand on the window. I put on a pair of sunglasses to hide my raw eyes.

The scenery on the drive to Seattle is breathtaking. Being alone and letting out all of my bottled up emotions is bringing me a sense of calm.

When I finally arrive, I sit in the car for a moment in silence. I turn my phone on just to call Dad and the girls to let them know I made it. I have every intention of turning it back off as soon as I'm done—I don't want any distractions, or to face the chance that Clay may call or text. I have twenty-three missed calls, all from him. I have seven text messages: five from Clay, one from Eric, and one from Rose. I ignore everything except the message from Rose; she just asks if I'm doing OK on the drive. I text her back and tell her I'm here and I am.

I walk in the door of Aunt Meg's, and it's quiet. My aunt informed me she and Becca will be back later today, and to make myself at home. No one knows about the baby or my loss, except my sisters. I just told Dad and Aunt Meg that Clay and I had a bad breakup, and I needed to get away for a bit. I'm not sure how long I will stay—I planned for the rest of the week, but I may never go back.

I carry my bags into the spare room and lie on the bed to rest—doctor's orders. I'm exhausted from the lack of sleep and the stress that has eclipsed me.

My mind won't shut off and the thoughts of last week keep circling in my brain. Two important pieces of my heart have been ripped away from me like the branch of a tree on a windy day—fast, painful, and destructive. If I thought I was strong before, I'll be invincible if I survive this.

My eyes are heavy, I shut them until the weight is lifted, and I'm dreaming about him and when life was simple, just a couple short weeks ago. The thought of just ending all the pain and going with Mom crossed my mind briefly, but I prayed and knew that God set this all in motion for a reason—I'm still here for a reason.

The voices of Aunt Meg and Becca in the other room wake me up. I lie still for a few minutes, and then go out to greet them.

Aunt Meg wraps her arms around me and tells me that I'm welcome to stay as long as I'd like. Becca tells me that there are some great parties this week and I figure that I'll have to tell her what happened so she can understand more of what I'm going through. I trust my cousin, as far as secrets go.

I spend the next few of days resting and relaxing. Becca and I watch the whole series of *One Tree Hill*. I apply for a position working on the *Watchdog* newspaper at Bellevue; it doesn't pay, but I'd get course credit for my time if I get it. On top of that, I apply for a paying job in the bookstore. Now I just wait, and see if any of it pans out.

I'm pretty sure that my miscarriage has passed and my hormones are slowly returning to normal. I still haven't returned any calls or messages from anyone except my family. I haven't logged on Facebook in almost a week, and I still don't think I'm ready to talk to anyone significant in my life. Becca persuaded me into attending another party at the frat house from my last trip, and I feel like it may do me some good to get out. The nice thing about this party is that I don't know anyone and no one knows me, so I can create my own character to show them. The *real Iris* can take a rest for a while.

We spend the morning shopping and getting our nails done. Aunt Meg noticed how we'd been lying around all week and offered to buy us each a new outfit; I didn't even try to refuse this time. I buy a black form-fitting dress—much more revealing than I'm used to—and a pair of wedge shoes I may not be able to walk in. Becca says I look hot and I feel sexy in it.

"How do I look?" I do a spin for Becca after I put on my new dress. Becca's curled my hair, and the beach waves flow around my face.

"Yes!" she exclaims.

I grab the clutch purse I borrowed and we go outside, where Rex is lying on the horn; he doesn't stop until he sees us.

"Asshole." She swats his arm and slides into the passenger seat. I climb in the back, and realize there is a guy right next to me. It's Jackson.

Chapter Twenty Nine

CLAY

It's been six days since I've talked to Iris—six days that feel like an eternity. When I heard about the baby, I felt like I lost a part of me. No one will ever understand, partly because no one knows, but I did want that baby and I've had to grieve this loss all on my own. I could imagine playing catch with my son or protecting my daughter from boys like me; they wouldn't stand a chance. Iris and I were only together for a short amount of time, but I've known she was The One my whole life, and I know she still is. She has my heart and my soul and she took it with her when she left. Now I sit here, bitter and empty, just existing in a world full of pain.

I crack open another beer after I toss my empty can to the side. Being here at the lake—our spot—isn't the same without her. I always thought alcohol was supposed to dull the pain, but lately it just intensifies it. I've been drinking every day since she left. I lost my internship because I never showed up. I still haven't talked to my boss; I just ignore his calls. Eventually my dad will know, and he'll probably kick my ass out as well as cut off my tuition. I have no clue what each day will bring at this point, so I just go with the flow, day by day. Today it has brought me to this case of Bud Light.

My truck stereo is turned up to “Red Ragtop” by Tim McGraw; it makes me think of me and Iris. I try calling her again, just like every hour, in hopes of her finally answering. I don't even bother to leave another voicemail; I've left about twenty-five.

"Clay," I hear Bryce yell, but I don't even turn around to acknowledge him. "Dude, you've got to pull it together, man."

"What the hell do you want?" I take another drink of my Bud and stare out the lake.

"I want you to tell me what your deal is lately. This is the third time this week I've had to track you down, and every time you are sitting here at the lake, drunk and depressed. You don't answer my calls and your brother is getting worried about you." He kneels down in front of me.

"Luke doesn't give a shit about me."

"Yes, he does. He called me this morning and asked me to make sure you are OK. He said you've been moping around at home, all sad and shit."

"Luke can pretend he cares all he wants. I know better." I crush my empty beer can with my hands and then toss it and stand up. "I'm fine, man. Just a broken heart, nothing a few days and a few beers won't fix," I lie, knowing full-fledge that it will take a lifetime to get over Iris, and that the memory of losing our unborn child will stay with me forever. It's my fault; I stressed her out too much. I pushed her buttons that night and I probably hurt her so deeply that she lost the baby.

The worst part is: I wasn't there.

"I should have been there," I spit. "I should have fucking been there." I drop to my knees and my fists grip my hair as I pull and I feel like I am losing all control.

"Clay, man, what the hell happened? What are you talking about?"

"Iris. She was... she was pregnant, Bryce." I had to say it. I can't keep it to myself anymore. The pain is too deep and the secret is slowly eating away at everything left in me. If I don't tell someone, then I may do something I can't come back from.

"Oh, shit." Bryce places his hand on my shoulder.

"She lost the baby." I look up at him and I can see that he gets it now. "I told her I wanted her to have an abortion and then I went to your cabin and screwed everything up. I pushed her away and broke her heart and she went home and had a miscarriage. I wasn't there for her."

"Clay, this isn't your fault. There is nothing you could have done." He gets up and grabs us both a beer.

"Nothing you say or do will ever convince me that this isn't my fault. I will always blame myself, because I will never know otherwise."

"Where is Iris now?" He sits down next to me as I lean back on the tree.

"I don't know. Her family won't tell me. I haven't talked to her since the night at the cabin. Lily is the one who told me about the miscarriage— otherwise I wouldn't even know that." I shake my head in disappointment with myself.

"She'll come back, man, and when she does, I'm sure you'll work it out. You two are like something out of a romance novel. Honestly, at first I didn't get it, but after seeing you with her, I knew you loved her."

"I do, with everything in me. You really think we'll work it out?" I'm desperate for reassurance.

"Absolutely, just give it some time. And a little bit of advice: be ready for her. Drinking all day every day like this isn't doing anyone any good. Show her that you can be there for her from now on. Whatever you feel you need to do to make it up to her, do it."

He's right. I need to clean myself up and pull my shit together. She could be coming back any day and this isn't the person I want her to come home to.

"Thanks, Bryce." I pat his back. "Well, it's already eight o'clock so I don't think she's coming back tonight, so let's finish this case and I'll start fresh tomorrow." I laugh, and it almost feels foreign; I haven't laughed or smiled in a week.

Bryce and I reminisce at the lake for another hour and then he gives me a ride home; I'm too drunk to drive myself.

My parents are already in bed. Luke is on the couch, and I pause for a minute, then decide to go in and talk to him.

"Thanks for sending Bryce out to talk to me."

Luke can't believe the words that are coming out of my mouth, and I'm having a hard time wrapping my head around it, too.

"Yeah, I'm glad he found ya. Everything OK?" he asks.

"It will be."

I walk away, and with just that, I feel like we've made a huge leap in the right direction. It's time to let it go.

Alcohol gives us a mask to wear and when it's on, we can be whoever we want, say what we want, do what we want. But that mask always comes off, and when it does, we have to face the consequences. Luke faced his; now I have to face mine. I just hope I can forgive myself as I will one day forgive him.

"Hey, can you give me a ride to get my truck tomorrow?" I yell from the kitchen.

"Sure thing." He smiles and turns back to the T.V.

Chapter Thirty

IRIS

"Hello again," Jackson purrs from the backseat of Rex's car. It's dark and I can't see him well, but every now and then, I catch a glimmer of blue eyes.

"Hi." I smile and turn to face the front.

I become very conscious of those eyes on me as I sit with my hands in my lap. His gaze makes me uneasy in a delightful sort of way. I know it's only been a week since my life took an unexpected turn that changed me forever, but I need to feel alive again, and Jackson's attention on me is doing just that.

"Can I help you?" I ask, making it known that I see him watching me.

"Sorry, you just look stunning and I can't take my eyes off you."

I turn my head towards the window so that my response to his flattery isn't obvious.

"So, Iris," he says. "Tell me what you're all about."

"What I'm all about?"

"Sure, tell me about yourself. Where do you go to school, work, live? What do you like to do for fun?" He slides a little closer.

"Well, um... I'm from Leavenworth, I wait tables at a diner, and I'm going to school at Bellevue this fall."

"Bellevue, huh? So you'll be moving closer to me, then." He slides even closer.

The truth of his statement makes me blush, because I will indeed be living closer to him. I don't know why I feel so nervous. I suppose it's because when we first met, I was drinking and not over-thinking. Now I sit here thinking about the attraction I feel towards him and how wrong it is that I'm feeling this way.

"I suppose I will be." I smile and realize he is now sitting in the middle of the backseat, right next to me.

"Oh, I'm sorry. Am I too close? I couldn't see you." He inches back over towards the door.

"No, no. You're fine." I laugh.

We finally get to the party, and I am relieved to get out of the car and away from Jackson. Something about the way he makes me feel giddy and nervous worries me. I've never been drawn to anyone except Clay, this feeling has me trying to get away so I don't have to think about it.

I decide not to drink tonight, simply because I have no desire. Here I stand: that *awkward girl,* by herself in a room full of strangers, nothing I'm not used to. Becca is already throwing back the drinks and dancing in the living room. I go outside and sit to get some fresh air and quiet.

There are a lot of people outside, as well, but at least I can move without bumping into someone. I make my way over to a bench in the yard and sink down into it, crossing my legs. The music from inside fills my ears and the grass feels damp on my open-toed wedges. For a moment, I consider turning my phone on and listening to my voicemails, although I know it will bring the pain back to the surface. Thankfully, I am stopped.

"What is a pretty girl like you doing out here all alone?" Jackson takes a seat next to me, slouched down on the bench. I can see him more clearly now and he's wearing another baby-blue shirt that matches his eyes.

"I just needed some air." I uncross my legs and stick my hands under them.

"We've only been here for ten minutes," he laughs.

"That's true. I'm just not really in the mood to mingle with strangers tonight." Realizing how that sounds, I correct myself: "Not you—not that you are a stranger—I mean everyone else in the house."

"No, I get it. I have those nights, too. It's a lot to take in. I have to deal with this shit almost every day in the summer and it gets old after a while."

"Oh, you live here." I point to the house.

"Yep, this is my home away from home."

"So where is your real home?"

"Olympia, born and raised." He takes a drink of his beer and I just nod. "You seem down, is something bothering you?"

There is no way I am pouring my heart out to him. He may not consider himself a stranger but this frat boy is just that to me, even if I do feel like he would be a good listener.

"I'm fine, I should probably get back inside, though. Becca is probably wondering where I disappeared to." I stand up and tug at my dress a little bit to bring it down.

Back inside the house, everything is the same, except now Becca is sitting on Rex's lap on the couch. Jackson and I join them and we listen to stories about how Rex got into the fraternity. I find myself laughing when he shares that he had to go into the girl's fraternity butt-naked and they all tackled him to the ground. A streak of sadness chases my bout of laughter as I remember whom I left back at home.

We've been here for over an hour, now, but I really just want to go back to Aunt Meg's and get away from the crowd. Becca and Rex are pretty drunk, so Jackson offers to give me a ride, since he's been nursing one drink the whole time we've been here. I am unsure at first but he seems harmless—mysterious, but harmless. His attention on me made me uncomfortable at first, though I'm starting to feel a bit more at ease in his presence.

We get into Rex's car and pull away, and as the music slowly fades into the distance, we are left with silence. "Did you just want to get out of there, or do you really want to go home?" he asks.

"A little of both. I wasn't really feeling it tonight and I am sort of tired," I say as I twirl the string of my clutch around my finger.

"If you don't mind, I'd like to show you something." He looks over at me and my eyes catch his.

"Um... I don't know. I am pretty tired," I stutter.

"Don't worry, Iris, I would never hurt you." He chuckles. "It's a place I like to go when I need to get away and feel... well, like you look like you feel tonight."

I think for a moment and decide to go, against my better judgment. I nod.

We turn off the main road onto a side street that leads us to a narrow two-track, but it's not like the ones at home; it's more of a gravel drive. We drive all the way to the end and park next to a small outhouse. Jackson shuts off the car and I stay seated, thinking that this was probably a bad idea. He pulls out a small blanket from the back seat and puts it around his neck. He could be a murderer or a rapist and I'm out here in the middle of nowhere alone with him. I quickly struggle to pull out my phone and turn it on, just in case I need to call for help, then I stuff it back in my clutch. He opens my door and extends his hand and I take it in mine.

He looks down at my feet. "Probably not the best shoes for this, but we'll walk slow."

We continue to walk down a trail for a couple minutes as Jackson uses a flashlight to guide us. I stumble over a branch on the path and he braces my fall. He takes a hold of my hand

and it feels bigger and stronger than what I'm used to. Clay isn't small-framed by any means, but Jackson is very tall and muscular, and his hands are much larger than Clay's. They feel rough and resemble that of a hardworking man.

"What do you do for work?" I ask out of curiosity.

"I currently work at a music store but I'm majoring in Marketing with a minor in Fine Arts."

That didn't give me any clarification as to why his hands feel so rough, but once again, I am over-thinking things that are pointless.

We reach the end of the path, and I stop in awe. Directly in front of us is a huge mountain with a breathtaking waterfall. The sound of water flowing into the river is soothing, and I can see why Jackson would like to come here to escape the frat house.

"It's beautiful." I let go of his hand and walk closer. The light from the moon fills the whole river in front of me. The grass is so green and the water so clear.

"I thought you might like it." He walks over to me, pointing to a large rock at my left. "Sit here."

I shiver and rub my hands over my arms as I sit down, and Jackson wraps the blanket over my shoulders. I'm starting to feel more comfortable and have a tinge of guilt for doubting him. He informs me that he likes to come here and play his guitar, and the rough, calloused hands make sense to me now. We sit and talk about Jackson's childhood and he tells me how his parents used to drive here in the summers. He tells me about the observation deck and a campsite they'd stay at nearby, and how he met a girl there when he was fifteen and she showed him this place. He tells me she was the only girl he's ever had a relationship with, but she moved away to Florida, and the distance was too much strain.

Jackson asks a lot of questions about me, too, but most of my answers are *yes* and *no*. "I'm a pretty closed book," I admit.

"Can you answer one question?" He pulls the sliding blanket back on me.

"OK, one question."

"What did he do to you?"

"What do you mean? Who?"

"Your boyfriend. I can tell that someone hurt you and you are too gorgeous to be single."

"I did have a boyfriend." I look down. "But that's over now and it doesn't matter," I say, knowing that it does matter and the wound is still open and fresh.

I look up and Jackson's face is right next to mine, and when our lips touch, I don't stop him. Instead, I let the blanket fall to the ground and I slowly bring my hand up to his cheek as he wraps his fingers around the back of my neck underneath my hair. The kiss is hard and intense and I push my mouth deeper into his and the pain that I've felt this week fades into the distance.

My phone begins vibrating in my purse, and the sound breaks the seal of our lips.

"Do you need to get that?" Jackson asks.

I shake my head *no* and pull his face back to mine. I know this is wrong, but everything I have ever done has been right, and it feels good to be overstepping these boundaries I've set for myself for so long. It's just a kiss, after all—I would never allow it to get any further.

"That was um... nice," Jackson says as he moves his hands to my waist and licks his lips.

I turn my head and smile with my hands still on his shoulders. My phone begins vibrating again, and I don't even want to pull it out, because once I see Clay's name on the screen I'll be flooded with emotion. I reach my hand in the clutch and hold down the power button until the screen goes blank.

"You can answer it if you need to, I don't mind," Jackson assures me.

"It's no one important," I tell him. *Just the boy who stomped on my heart*, I think to myself.

Jackson and I walk along the river until we're closer to the waterfall, and he tells me that he's been writing music. I tell him I've done a little writing in the past, and he asks if I'd be willing to come by sometime offer my opinion on his work, and I agree. I give him my number and he says he will call me tomorrow. I'm not sure how much longer I plan on being in Seattle, but I'm supposed to go back to work in three days, so I have to make a decision.

The drive home is quiet and I try and wrap my head around the battle between my brain and my heart. My heart is telling me to go home to Clay and make things right. My brain is telling me to stay here and experience something new and exciting in the city. Either way, I will be coming back in just a few weeks for school.

Jackson pulls in to my aunt's driveway and says that he will talk to me tomorrow. I simply say thank you and get out of the car.

The house is quiet until Parker, their noisy little Yorkshire terrier, starts yapping. I shush him repeatedly so he doesn't wake up my aunt; I don't feel like explaining I left Becca at the party.

The next morning, I'm woken by a knock on the bedroom door. "Iris, is Becca in here?" Aunt Meg asks as she enters the room.

"No, she's not in her room?"

"She's not. Did she come home with you?"

"Umm... no, I was tired so I left early. She stayed with Rex." I pull myself up into a sitting position.

She shakes her head. "Rex, huh? I told her to stay away from that boy. All he does is drink and sleep."

"I'll shower and then take a ride over there and pick her up."

"Thank you, sweetie." She turns to walk out the door. "Oh, and Iris? Whatever is going on with you lately, remember: This, too, shall pass."

"Thanks, Aunt Meg."

This will pass—but I wish it were sooner rather than later. Every morning when I wake up, my thoughts go to him. I imagine him being here with me and seeing that smile on his face and his beautiful green eyes staring into my soul. I grab my phone off the nightstand and hold it for a minute before powering it on.

My main screen is a picture of Clay and me at the lake in front of our tree. Looking at the picture makes me think this is a bad idea. Countless text messages pop up but I close them; I can't read his messages yet. I have thirty-six missed calls. I decide to listen to my voicemail from Eric and he's just checking in to make sure I'm OK. The last time I talked to Eric, he was dropping me off at home in tears because of what Clay did at the cabin. I send him a quick message apologizing again for that night and tell him I'm out of town temporarily, but I'm fine.

Another voicemail, from a number I don't recognize:

"Iris, um... hey. It's Bryce. Listen, I know I haven't always been a decent person to you and I'm sorry for that. The reason I'm calling is because Clay is a mess without you. I'm not saying that you should forgive him, but at least hear him out. He's hurting, too. I know about everything and he's trying to be a better person for you. Just think about it."

I'm not upset that he shared this information with Bryce. I told my sisters because I needed someone to confide in, and he should be able to do the same. It doesn't change the fact that I don't feel badly for his pain right now. He *should* be hurting. What he did in those two days completely destroyed us, and we will never be able to go back and make it right. I know that losing the baby wasn't his fault, but instead of being there for me, he was with another girl, drunk and incoherent. Even if I tried telling him what was going on that night, he wouldn't have been in the right mind to give me the support I needed.

Anger rises in me. Maybe because Bryce's message was all about Clay, and I'm sure he is probably making this all about him. For once, I am thinking of myself and doing what I have to do to get better.

I decide that is enough going through my phone for the day and shut it back off, but then quickly turn it back on. I find Facebook, and I change my status to *single*.

When I get to the frat house, I just walk in, since the door is halfway open. A couple of guys are in the kitchen picking up bottles and cups and throwing them in a trash bag.

"I'm looking for Becca and Rex," I say to a short blond.

"They must still be asleep. Haven't seen them." He carries on with what he's doing. I pull out my phone to call Becca when Jackson appears.

"Iris, what a nice surprise." He smiles.

"Hey, Jackson. Do you know where Becca is?" I look around at all the mess and it's much worse than when I left last night. The house looks odd without all the bodies moving through it.

"They're still asleep and I imagine they will be for a while. They were still going strong when I got back here at one a.m."

"Ugh, OK. Well, will you have her call me when she wakes up? I'll come get her."

"Sure, or you can just hang out. I was gonna call you soon anyways and see if you wanted to look at my music."

"I, um. I guess I could do that," I figure. It's not like I have much else to do.

I follow Jackson up the stairs and he opens up a door that I assume is his bedroom. It's much different than I would imagine in a frat house. The walls are covered with posters of music notes, guitars, and a few pictures of some bands I don't recognize. In find myself staring at one because the name sounds familiar.

"You heard of him?" he asks, glancing from me to the poster.

"Beck? It sounds familiar, but I don't think so."

"He's my idol. Beck encouraged me to write my own music after I saw his live tour in Miami when I was thirteen."

"Oh, so you've been writing for awhile?"

He walks over to his neatly organized desk and pulls out a very thick notebook, which he then hands to me. I flip through; it's completely full of songs he wrote. "Wow," I murmur. "I guess so."

"This is the one that I just finished and I need some advice on." He turns to the back while I still hold it in my hands.

"May I?" I look at the bed.

"Of course, sit down." He walks over and moves a couple pillows to the top of the bed.

I read his song, “Bittersweet Despair,” and it speaks to me. It's about a boy falling in love and how it took him by surprise and swept him away like the wind of a hurricane. His feelings so real and so deep, and then he’s drowned by the feeling of losing that love, having to move on without her. How each day is a struggle until each day becomes a triumph because he's making it and he's OK.

"Is this about her? The girl you told me about last night?" I ask, looking over at him and he just nods.

"Thank you for letting me read this. It's good, really good. I'd love to hear you play it."

I'm impressed with his ability to let just anyone read his music. I've always been very private with my writing. Jackson must have a different level of confidence in his craft, and he should, because it's very good. He fetches his guitar and sits down on the edge of the bed.

His voice is just as incredible as his writing, and the way he strings his guitar makes him even more attractive than he already was to me. I sit and listen, closing my eyes for a moment to take it all in. She was a lucky girl to have him; he truly loved her. It's unfortunate that time and distance tore them apart, but that tends to happen with everything you love. Nothing good lasts forever, as far as I can see. We can feel happiness in one moment and the next moment feel sadness and the event that brought the smile or filled your heart with joy eventually becomes a memory.

He stops playing and takes a deep breath and looks at me, waiting for my thoughts.

"That was amazing, Jackson. Really, I could feel it in here." I pat my chest. "You have a lot of talent."

"You think so?" He smiles from ear to ear.

"I know so."

Something about being in Jackson's presence feels peaceful and calm; he's a distraction from everything. I find myself wanting to be around him more, so I take him up on his offer to go get lunch. He tells the guys downstairs to let Becca know that I'll be back.

Chapter Thirty One

CLAY

It's been two months since Iris left. The pain has eased, and I'm beginning to accept that she may not be coming back before she starts school. I miss her every day, but I have to live my life and better myself for her and the possibility that she may return.

Bryce and most all of the college students here have returned to school, so the town is quiet and uneventful.

My dad and I had a very tough but meaningful conversation, and I was honest with him—somewhat. I told him that I don't want to return to Washington State. I wasn't excelling there; all I did was party and my grades were undesirable. I was a bit taken aback when he supported my decision.

Instead, I've been working for Mr. Everly. The pay isn't the best, but it's nice to be someplace familiar, and I've always enjoyed the good vibes at the farm; the Everlys are such kind people, to us and to the community. He gave me the job under one condition: I can't ask about Iris. I've held up my end of the deal for the most part, but once in a while, I'll try to sneak in a question when I think he or the twins are off-guard. They don't budge. Mr. Everly says she happy and that's enough for me, for now.

I signed up for the Conservation Office Academy to become a conservation officer, and will be leaving next week for the nineteen-week program in Portland. I was really hoping to see Iris before I left, but I do get a couple weekend breaks in-between, so maybe I'll get lucky and she will home during one.

The wind is blowing pretty hard today. I back my truck up to the lake and put down the tailgate and open my book—her book. I've been reading it every day and I've finally caught up to this summer.

Sitting on my bed, I look out my window and see the oak I planted when I was five years old that sets between my house and the farm. I remember watching it day after day and becoming so discouraged when it didn't grow. Eventually, I stopped paying attention to it, and it grew. Now it is this big beautiful tree with so many branches and leaves. I wonder if I stop thinking so much about growing up and my future if it will just happen. One day at a time, the way it's meant to be.

Iris's wisdom never ceases to amaze me. I wonder if I stop thinking so much about her coming back if it will just happen, the way it's meant to be.

I feel so safe and content in his arms and I don't want to let go. Clay holds me for what feels like minutes, and what I sense inside of myself scares me a little bit.

I know exactly what it was: love. I felt it, too, and I still do. She was scared to fall and I told her to never be afraid of loving me. I made a promise to myself that I would never hurt her and I let us both down. If I'd just left her alone at the beginning like I planned, then she would have never been hurt. I figured it was time for us to be together—maybe my timing was wrong. Maybe if I had waited one more year, I would've gotten it right.

I read a few more chapters and decide to head home when the sun begins to set. The house is as quiet; Luke is back at school and my parents are at a township meeting. I try and call Iris, and lately—instead of it going straight to voicemail—it rings before her voice comes on the recording.

"Hey, it's Iris. I can't get to the phone, so leave a message and I'll call you back."

What a load of shit. I leave her a message every single night and she's never called me back. I continue to try, though.

"Iris, it's me again. I just want you to know that I'm still thinking about you. Time will never change how much I love you. One day, I will prove that to you. Sleep my tight, my love."

The boy in me has wanted to chase her down every day since she has left. I now know that she's been in Seattle. The man in me says that she will come back to me when she's ready, so I need to give her the time she needs.

There are a few pages ripped out of the book. I imagine this is when Iris started writing what she said she wanted. She must have torn them out and continued to write our real-life memories.

I read the final pages of the book, and reality hits me that once I'm done, I have nothing left to remind me of her—except the memories.

My heart stops when I get to the last page.

Clay,

If you are on this page, then that means you are all caught up to the present day. Unless you skipped ahead—you better not have, or I'll kick your butt.

These past few weeks have been nothing short of magical. I never knew my heart could hold so much love for one person. It is my hope and dream that we have continued to build on the foundation that was set for us when we were only children. Children with wild imaginations, no sense of responsibility, and dreams that felt out of reach. Because of you, my dreams are not as far away as I had thought. Most people dream of being successful and powerful; I dreamed of you. Thank you for allowing me to open my heart and showing me that not everyone you love leaves you. Thank you for loving me.

All my love,

Iris

"I'm sorry I let you down."

I say it out loud, even though she can't hear me.

Chapter Thirty Two

IRIS

The drive back to Leavenworth seems longer than usual. It's been two months since I left.

School has been a nice distraction and I'm enjoying my classes. I can't wait to see Dad. I've never left home for this long before. When I left Leavenworth, I was broken—going back, I am healing. I still have a way to go before I am whole again but I am getting there, one day at a time.

I pull into my driveway and text Jackson to let him know I made it. Jackson and I have been seeing each other for a couple of weeks now. He's such a gentleman and has a way of making me feel at ease. We aren't serious at all, but I enjoy his company.

I plan on calling Clay while I'm home. Dad told me that he's leaving tomorrow for the academy. I need to see him one last time so that I can have the closure I desperately need.

I was never able to bring myself to listen to his voicemails or read his text messages. I deleted them all. Every night, I would sit and wait just to see his name appear on my screen, only to disappear. Last week, I waited and waited and he never called—he hasn't tried again. He probably thinks I ignore him because I hate him. The truth is, it's the complete opposite. I knew that I had to be strong enough before I could face him again. If I wasn't, then I would go back, and I wouldn't have had this opportunity to find myself again.

I'm only in town for the weekend since I have to get back to my classes on Monday. Becca and I were able to get a room in the residence halls, and even though we aren't right by my sisters, we're right down the road and that is comforting. The twins brought a carload of my belongings when they came back, but there are a few special things I still need to grab.

"Dad!" I run into his arms as he walks out the door. "I've missed you so much."

"I've missed you, too, honey." He wraps his arms around me tightly; his touch and smell remind me of home. Leavenworth will always be home.

Dad and I spend some time catching up. I tell him all about my new job at the school bookstore and how I will also be writing for the school newspaper. I can tell he was caught off-guard when I told him that I am seeing someone—he almost seemed sad for me instead of happy. I know that he and Clay have gotten close this past month, and I'm sure that part of him hoped we would work it out.

"Hi, sweetie," Donna says as she walks into the kitchen and puts her arms around my shoulder.

I smile. "Donna, hi. It's great to see you."

"Iris, Donna and I planned on going out for dinner. I was hoping you would join us."

"No thanks, Dad. I have a few errands I have to run and some calls to make. Popcorn and movie tonight?"

"It's a date," he says as he puts his arm around Donna and leads her out the door.

I go into my room and pack up a few more things I need to bring to school with me, reaching into the closet top shelf and pulling down a plastic bag. After throwing on Mom's black sweater to armor myself from the chill in the air, I load all of my things into the trunk of my car, but I can't seem to put the plastic bag inside.

I retreat to the porch steps and peek inside, and—knowing this is going to sting—I reach in and I pull out the yellow booties I bought for my baby. I hold them against my chest and the memory of that day returns. Tears fill my eyes and I look up and take a deep breath when I see him.

"Clay." My heart sinks into my chest. I wipe the tears away and I stick the booties back into the bag. "What are you doing here?"

His hair is longer now and the stubble on his face makes it obvious that he hasn't shaved in some time, but those eyes—those eyes are still as enticing as ever.

"Were those for the baby?"

"Yeah, I bought them before... well, you know. It was stupid. I never should have bought something for him so early on."

"Him?"

"Oh, I don't know if it was a boy. But when I picture him in my head, he is." I look away and hope we can change the subject because I don't want to talk about this, or feel this.

"I'm sorry to just show up. I was over at the farm and your dad said you'd be home this weekend. I saw your car and figured I'd bring you this." He hands me my notebook.

"My notebook. I forgot all about this. I've been so busy that I..."

"Lost track of yourself?" He cuts me off and sticks his hands in the pockets of his blue jeans.

"No, no, I didn't lose track of myself. I was finding myself." I stand up and suddenly feel very defensive.

"Really? Because the Iris I know loved to write."

I scoff. This isn't going at all like I planned. "I still do, I just haven't had time lately. Anyway, that doesn't matter. I was going to call you."

"It does matter, Iris." He sits down on the step.

"I haven't talked to you in months and you want to tell me that I've lost myself. Maybe I have changed, Clay. Maybe I needed to change. I was this quiet and vulnerable girl and it brought me nowhere," I shout.

"It brought you to me." He looks into my eyes and I turn away almost instantly. I don't want him to see the tears.

"And look how that turned out."

I feel his hand on my shoulder and he turns me around. "Don't ever be afraid to cry in front of me." He wraps his arms around me and I melt into him.

"Clay, I'm seeing someone," I say without thinking first. I had planned to tell him, though I wasn't sure how; this seemed like a good moment, but now I wish I could take it back.

He pulls away and the anguish I just caused is written all over his face. Clay backs up and sits back down on the porch step and buries his face in his hands.

"I didn't plan to tell you like this. I'm sorry, Clay. We gave it our best shot but we couldn't make it work. I have no regrets and you will always have a special place in my heart." I sit down next to him and put my hand on his arm, but he pulls it away abruptly.

"I have to go." He gets up and walks towards his truck.

"Clay, wait. It wasn't supposed to be like this," I yell as I chase after him and the tears begin falling again. "Clay, please."

And just like that, he's gone.

If he only knew how I really felt deep down inside. My heart wanted to scream, I'm in here, Clay. I love you, please come back to me. I need you and I miss you. There will never be anyone else for me, you have my heart, please keep it safe for me. My head wouldn't let her speak, like sisters at battle to get in the last word. I can't be vulnerable anymore. I can't allow myself to fall again.

I pick up my book and go back in the house.

Chapter Thirty Three

CLAY

She's seeing someone. It's only been two months—how has she even met anyone else already? I get in my truck and I drive. I have no destination in mind but I heard towards the mountains and I don't stop. My heart is plummeting out of my chest and I can't think clearly right now. I had hoped that today would be a new beginning for us.

I pull into a corner pub in a small town outside of Leavenworth.

"You look like you could use a drink. What'll it be?" the bartender asks.

I had only intended to grab a quick bite to eat, but since she's not questioning my age at all, I go with it. "Jack and Coke, make it a double."

The pub is pretty run down. Dust fills the tops of liquor bottles behind the bar and the green of the pool table is faded to a yellow.

I finish my second drink and slide the empty glass home. "I'll take another."

The jukebox in the corner is old and I walk over to flip through. Most of the albums are classics, but there are a few modern-day collections. "It's free play," the bartender calls.

I go back to my stool and order another drink. The sappy country music mixed with the scenery really feeds my fucked-up emotions.

Iris has moved on. It's really over this time. I feel this immense void and emptiness inside and nothing will ever be able to fill it, except her. I could go back—I could go right now and fight for her. But she doesn't want me anymore. She doesn't love me anymore. I always thought I'd be her first and her last and the idea of another man taking her to bed sends an enormous ache to my already broken heart.

"So, what's got you down?" The bartender leans forward. The bar is empty now, and I imagine she's getting pretty bored wiping the counters back and forth. She could go dust the cobwebs in the corners or run a broom around the dirty floors, but instead, she focuses on me.

"Life." I look up at her.

"I see a lot of broken-hearted men pass through this town and ninety percent of the time it's because of a girl." She makes me another drink, and slides it over. "This one's on me. So, lover boy, what's her name?"

I take the drink in one big gulp and slam the glass down to the bar. "Iris."

"Ahh, so it is a girl. Iris must be with someone new."

She's good, I'll give her that. She must do this a lot. "Yep. I've lost her forever."

"Nothing lasts forever. If it's meant to be, it will. Time has a way of proving that to us."

"Time." I laugh. I'm leaving tomorrow for the next four months and while I'm gone, I won't be able to fight for her; she'll continue to get close to her new guy and I'll just be a thing of the past.

"Iris would argue that time means change and that change is what tears people apart." I shake my head.

"Clever girl. However, Iris might not know yet that time and change are the only things that are constant."

I sit and think about what she just said. We can't stop time; therefore, we cannot prevent change. Iris has always tried to come off as strong, but I'm the only one who knows how scared she really is. Maybe she does still love me; maybe she's just reluctant because part of her thinks that it won't last.

"I have to go talk to her." I stand up and stumble backwards but catch myself.

"Whoa. You do, but not tonight, cowboy." She rushes over to me and places her hand on back to brace my fall.

"You don't understand, I'm leaving tomorrow and she's leaving and I have to go, I have to go now." I lean onto the old pool table.

"I get it, I do. But I can't let your drive. You'll have to sober up first or call an Uber."

"I'll call her. Maybe she'll come." It's not likely, because she hasn't answered a single call in the last thirty-five days, but it's worth a shot.

Her voicemail picks up.

"Iris, it's Clay. I need to see you. We need to talk. I can't leave things like this. Can you come pick me up in..."

"Here, give me the phone." She grabs the phone from me.

"Hello, Iris. This is Sherri. Clay is at Rocky's Pub in Waterville. He's had a tad too much to drink and I can't let him drive, so if you could come get him, he'd appreciate it."

She hands me the phone back and I hang up. This was pointless—she's not going to come. She won't even listen to the voicemail. I sink down into a chair at small black table. I decide to try texting her with a small amount of hope left inside me.

Iris, please, call me. I need to see you. I need to tell you everything that I failed to say to you this summer.

Sherri places a basket of fries and an ice water in front of me. "You tried." She smiles.

I slam the water and my only chance of getting out of here is sobering up for next couple hours or calling my dad, and that's not happening.

"Yeah," I agree, and sigh. "It's never good enough, though."

Chapter Thirty Four

IRIS

"Thanks for helping me with this," I tell Mr. Radley as he pounds in the second post for the sign. "My dad is going to love it."

"No problem, Iris. I'm so glad you were able to get the farm back. This sign should have never been taken down." He shakes his head as if he wishes he never changed the name.

"Well, it's back now, and that's all that matters." I smile and I screw in the hooks. Then I lift the sign up and hang it on the white wooden posts. "Everly Place," I say as we both stand back and admire the fresh varnish.

Mr. Radley places a hand on my shoulder. "Just as it should be."

I walk down to the main barn where I told Dad to stay put, and I have him follow me up the drive. He's frowning. "I can't believe you already have to leave tomorrow," he sighs.

"I know. The weekend went too fast. We'll all be home in two months for Thanksgiving, though." I lean my head onto his shoulder as we walk.

And then, we're there.

"Ta-da!" I say, gesturing my hands to the sign.

"Oh, Iris. It's perfect. I was wondering where that old sign went. I looked in the shed for hours and couldn't find it. Everly Place." Dad crosses his arms and smiles in silence as he takes in the view of the sign with the farm behind it. Then he walks over and wraps his arms around me.

"Thank you, honey." He kisses my head and I'm grinning from ear to ear. This is what I've always wanted for Dad. He has his farm back, he's found love again, and he's simply happy.

Happiness is an overused word, but it's an also an overlooked emotion. We can find happiness is the smallest of things and in the biggest encounters. People come in and out of our lives and leave us with only the imprint that they make on hearts. I'm fortunate enough to have had many moments of happiness, and they surpass the moments of sadness by far. Everything that has happened has brought me to this significant point in my life where I am finally finding myself and waiting for my undeniable happiness to peak. I am far from it, but until then, I'll find happiness in the small things along the way.

I go into my room and sit on my bed in silence and look around at the walls and into the memories of my childhood, my awkward coming of age years, and now my adult years. My pink curtains still hang in the same spot they've been since I was eleven; my white jewelry box sits on the vanity Mom got me when I was eight and it now holds her beautiful white wedding day pearls. What stands out the most, though, is the collage of pictures on my cork board. I walk over and study them. The photos begin when I was a little girl—there's me and Clay building a blanket fort in the living room, my sisters and I braiding each other's hair in a row on the floor, my one shot at basketball when I was nine. With each year, each picture develops more and more, a perk of high definition technology. The oldest one is faint and weathered; it's a picture of Mom and Dad kissing in the kitchen. The newest one is Clay and me taking a selfie at the lake, and it is bright and crisp— flawless, rather. I take the two pictures into my hand and sit at the end of my bed, observing them.

Mom and Dad were so happy and so in love. She's not here, but he never actually lost her, or lost that love. Her memory still fills his heart with the same happiness it always has. Maybe time doesn't have to take away from us. Maybe change doesn't always have to be a bad thing. Change is essential to get from one weathered photo to the next, and finally, to the clear and vivid picture. Time will continue to change the way the photos look— someday they will be even brighter—but that's life. Life is a continuous change, and you have to take the old with the new.

I grab my notebook off my nightstand and flip through the pages that hold my deepest thoughts and my most vivid memories. I read the letter that I wrote to Clay in the end and it makes me smile. He brought me to life; I didn't lose him; he was a page in my book that brought me to the next chapter, the next photo, and allowed me to find myself. As I shuffle through the pages a loose paper falls into my lap. I open it up and read it to myself.

My Dearest Iris,

You are a blinding ray of sunshine on a cloudy day. Since we were kids, I have been blinded by your beautiful soul and swept away by your grace. You deserve so much happiness and I truly hope that you have found that. 'I'm sorry' doesn't begin to make up for the pain that I have caused you. I know that we are no longer together because of my foolish actions I know that our baby would be growing inside you if I hadn't pushed you to your limit.

"No," I say out loud. My heart begins to swell at the thought of him blaming himself this whole time we've been apart. "It's not your fault, Clay."

I waited so long to call you mine and when I finally had your heart in the palm of my hands, I crushed it. I love you more than you will ever know. I always have and I always will, that will never CHANGE. If I can give you one thing to walk away from this relationship with it will be the ability to smile through the bad and love through the pain, open your heart to new things and find happiness in everything that comes your way.

Love,

Clay

I stand up as the letter falls slowly to the carpet.

I have to find him.

Chapter Thirty Five

CLAY

As I'm packing up my bag to leave my house for the academy, I'm reminded of the day I left for college last fall. It feels like it was just yesterday, yet so much has happened in-between those few short months.

I had everything planned out for myself: Graduate high school, go to college for four years, and get a job as a marine biologist. I've always known I wanted to work with nature, but I never expected to take this sharp of a turn and quit school. I suppose it's because Dad had it instilled in our heads that if we didn't go to college, then we would never be successful. His measure of success is different than mine. I look at a person like Mr. Everly and see more success in him than I do my own father, the mayor.

I'm pleasantly surprised that Dad handled the news of my decision so well.

When Dad started running for Mayor of Leavenworth, he sat my brother and I down and explained the importance of self image and how we had to show the community that we are an upstanding family. I think that was the day I changed. I was no longer the boy who ran barefoot through the mud; I was the boy who sat idly by, behaving while the other children ran amuck.

After that day, I had to think of Dad and how my actions would affect his career or how much of a disappointment I would be if I got a bad grade, or got caught drinking at the Friday night bonfires at the lake. I'm well-aware that being raised to have the utmost respect for adults and the knowledge to make good choices isn't a bad thing. I just wanted to make typical teenage bad choices—just out of spite—and sometimes I did, but I never got caught.

If Dad hadn't won the election, we would have continued to live out our simple life under the radar. Dad would have continued to teach high school math, and Mom would have still waited tables at the diner. I would have stayed next to Iris, in our small two-bedroom house with the rickety staircase and screen door that never latched shut. I never wanted the change and I would have been perfectly fine staying there and continuing to be a kid instead of being forced into acting like a man at the age of twelve.

Of all of the things that I lost during that change, Iris's friendship was by far the greatest. I'd trade the big house and nice vehicles to go back and catch frogs in the lake with her any day.

"Hey." Bryce pops his head in my room. "you busy?"

"No, just finishing up my packing. Heading out pretty soon." I tell him as I zip up my duffle bag.

Bryce takes a seat on my bed, picking up the picture of Iris and me and holding it in his hands.

"How are you two?"

I shake my head. "It's over, man."

"Damn. I'm sorry to hear that."

I don't want Bryce's pity, although I know he's trying to be a good friend.

"It is what it is." I sit down next to him and he hands me the picture.

"Well, you both gave it your best shot."

I look at us, so carefree and in love, in this picture.

"No," I shake my head. "We didn't."

"What do you mean? You tried everything, but if it's not meant to be, then it's not meant to be."

"We didn't give it our best shot. We gave up. Shit got hard and we gave up." I set the picture back down.

I've learned over the last couple months that Iris and I have more in common than I thought. We are both stubborn as hell and we both have a problem with speaking up when there are plenty of words to be said. We shut people out because, when we do, they can no longer hurt us. The truth is, whether right down the road or a hundred miles away, the pain will still be there. I'll never get over this loss.

"It's not our time, not yet," I tell him as I stand up to retrieve my bag from the floor.

"Maybe it never will be."

"Maybe you're right. All I know is I have nothing left to give right now. Only time will tell."

"Alright, Keller. Take it easy and don't let that sergeant boss you around too much." Bryce laughs.

"I don't think I have much of a choice. I'll see ya at Thanksgiving break."

When Bryce leaves, I take one more look around the room before hitting the lights and closing my door.

It's time to start a new journey and see where it takes me.

Chapter Thirty Six

IRIS

I rush down the stairs and into the living room and out the front door as fast as I can.

"Slow down, girl," Dad says as I nearly knock him over.

"Dad!" I stop as I catch my breath. "What time is Clay leaving?"

"Um..." He looks at his watch. "He's probably left by now, honey. If you hurry, you may be able to catch him."

"I have to, Dad. He can't leave." I run to my car and drive to the house as fast as I can.

It's just my luck that I get stuck behind a damn tractor at the end of my road. I lie on the horn until he pulls off to the side. "Thank you," I yell out my window, shameless, and wave with a smile.

I have to tell him it's not his fault and that I love him. He needs to know that I have accepted the changes that take place with the passing of time and that I get it now. He needs to know I will do whatever is necessary to make this work.

CLAY

"This is the last bag," Mom says as she shuts the back door of my truck. She puts her arms out and I go in for a hug. "I'm proud of you, son. Call me as soon as you get there." She kisses my forehead.

"It's only three hours away, Mom," I laugh and she gives me a serious look. "I'll call you."

Dad comes out and we all say our goodbyes. I'll be home in two months for Thanksgiving, and then two more months and I'll finish the academy and go on to take the state test before I'm officially a conservation officer for the DNR.

"I love you both," I say to my parents as they head back to the house

I hear the front door close when they go in and Luke walks out.

“Hold up,” he shouts, walking towards me. “Take it easy, bro.”

“Thanks, Luke.” I put my arm around him and pull him in for a hug as he pats my back.

“I’ll see ya soon,” he says as he walks away.

I smile and shake my head. “Yes, you will.”

I sit in the truck for a second and think about last night. Iris never came. I'm not sure if she didn't get my messages or if she just didn't care, but I sat at the pub for two hours hearing about Sherri's divorce and how she got custody of their hound dog before I finally felt sober enough to drive home.

On the drive home, I came to peace with our ending. We tried and we failed. I did all that I could do, and unfortunately, it wasn't enough for either of us.

I put the truck in reverse, look back in my rearview mirror, and see a car pulling in.

"Iris?"

To Be Continued...

About the Author

Rachel Kirwin has three beautiful children with her husband of 10 years. She enjoys relaxing at the beach, spending time with her family, and writing.

As a young child, Rachel was always conjuring up stories and filling them with colorful characters, sharing them with anyone and everyone who would listen. Since then, she's progressed quite a bit to formulating longer and more complex stories with the hope of sharing them with much larger audiences.

Made in the USA
Middletown, DE
26 June 2019